CEDAR GROVE

Stories

TOM REED

outskirtspress
DENVER, COLORADO

Cedar Grove
Stories
All Rights Reserved.
Copyright © 2014 Tom Reed
v2.0

Cover Photo © 2014 thinkstockphotos.com. All rights reserved - used with permission.

Outskirts Press, Inc.
http://www.outskirtspress.com

ISBN: 978-1-4787-4085-8

Outskirts Press and the "OP" logo are trademarks belonging to Outskirts Press, Inc.

PRINTED IN THE UNITED STATES OF AMERICA

Prologue

Everyone has a story. Some may seem more interesting than others throughout time. Some seem to have had easy, hard, happy, or tragic lives. Some mixed all elements together in one life. We remember tragic ones like JFK, Lincoln, and Martin Luther King. We remember ones with lots of publicity like Elvis, Babe Ruth, and Marilyn Monroe. Then there was Jesus. Most lives are more common. Actually each life is uncommon-- special.

This book is a collection of stories. It is built around an uncommon one of a farming family I named the Pattersons. The family is really one right next door to Cedar Grove, TN where most of these stories are based on fictional characters.

Cedar Grove could be anywhere rural America. It happens to be in rural West Tennessee about thirty miles northeast of Jackson and about halfway between

Memphis and Nashville. It is not a specifically defined area, unincorporated, rests on a relatively high ridge for that area of the state and is distinguished by rolling hills, which is different than the flat cotton land sloping to the west towards the Mississippi River. It is good land for cattle and small row crops. Confederate General Nathan Bedford Forest taunted the Union forces around West Tennessee and galloped through this land with his "hit and run" tactics disrupting their supply lines.

Jimmy and Jimbo Patterson (not their real names) are the core characters. Their uncommon story is real, but I have taken the liberty to add fiction to it and add other characters and their stories too. The book will jump from one story to the next, and back and forth through time, so I hope you won't be confused. I met the real Jimmy Patterson when I decided to leave the small town of Jackson, TN and buy some land in the country. I then leased the land to Mr. Patterson and heard his story. In the book, I'm John Sloan.

All the characters' time line go from 1790 to 2010. The 220 years cover the joys, and tragedies of uncommon common Americans living off our uncommon land.

The Pattersons are now very big and successful farmers in this section of the state, but it didn't start out that way....

Pattersons

The sweet, fertile, Tennessee, black dirt filtered through his fingers. He grabbed another handful, packed it in a ball then let it sift through his fingers again. He could smell the potential in it for growing cotton. The sun was warming his back from the chill of the morning. His thoughts remained with the soil.

Mother Earth.

This soil would care for his family as long as he did his part to care for it. Promises were made. Prayers silently sent.

Prayer.

As Jimmy looked over the 625 acres of his farm, he realized how much dirt he had to take care of. At 23, with a young wife and a baby, he felt the weight of doing things right.

Do right.

The moist dirt left marks on his knees as he

straightened up. He arched his back to relieve some of the stiffness, and inhaled the morning air. The cool breeze was confused with a mixture of morning dew and the smoke from last night's fire.

He turned his back on the 625 acres and began to make his way back to the house that lay before him, smoldering. His childhood home was no more than a huge heap of ashes. Jimmy was powerfully built from a combination of genetics and years of hard work and athletics. He had a mischievous glint in his eyes, but he was also a man with whom you didn't want to argue or tangle. His mother stood off to the side looking as the firemen worked their way through the debris seeking her husband. She knew he was dead. She and her son had heard the screams.

The house had served the family well. The house was white, two storied, weathered, with chimneys at each end. It had been added on to over the years, but retained its original character as a useful farm home. It contained the history of all the combined families. It held who they were and from Whom they came. There were also current treasures: Little league ball gloves, Barbie dolls, 4-H trophies, and pictures. The Bible, the porch swing. Memories.

It had needed paint, and that was going to be an early Spring project before planting time took all the time. Four children had grown up in it, and now a grandchild was going to learn how to navigate the front steps. The old house was near 100 years old, and had sheltered other generations before she and her husband had their turn on the farm. The land and the house had served them well. The reliance now would have to be on the land,

Mother Earth.

No one knew where or how the fire had started last night a few hours after they had gone to bed. Jimmy had left them around seven at the kitchen table. He ambled back to where he and his wife had a trailer, or manufactured home, set about a hundred yards from the "big house."

The night followed a familiar pattern. Supper, dishes, and on warm nights, a few moments outside on the porch swing to enjoy the night sounds. Jimmy's mother, Emily, particularly liked the time on the swing. Often she and her husband, Jim, Sr., would hold hands and listen to the nightly symphony of frogs, owls, assorted birds, a cow in the distance, and sometimes the calls of coyotes across the pastures. It was a peaceful time to talk the day out, and get ready for the sleep ahead. Jim anchored his side of the swing, and her life.

Jim woke first. He was always the light sleeper and keeper of the cave. He was a look-out during WWII until he was wounded and sent home, so he seemed to sleep with all his senses alert. If there was a hint of danger, he was the one to sense it first. He rolled over and woke her. "Get out of the house, fast," he had yelled. That jolted her to find her robe. That is all she had now. One tattered old robe he had bought her for a Christmas present years ago. The next few minutes were chaos. They both launched themselves down the stairs as the smoke was billowing up to meet them. The first floor was full of smoke and they felt heat. Passing through the kitchen screen door she heard the familiar bang of the door as it closed behind them. That screen door was part of the family history of sounds. Children coming and going created that sound. Emily felt the cold next. Jim led her to the big oak tree out front and out of danger.

"Go get Jimmy and call the fire department," he yelled for the second time that night. Emily started running. Her bare feet got wet from the dew, and she never felt the acorns under foot or soon, the gravel on the drive. As she was pounding on Jimmy's back door, her husband was going back into the kitchen with the screen door banging behind him.

Volunteer fire departments out in the country have good intentions, but by the time they get to most fires the structure is a total loss. Most of what they end up doing is watering the surrounding grass to keep the fire contained to one spot. Tonight was no different. The damage was done before they got there.

"No I don't know what he went back in for." Emily was talking to both Jimmy and the Cedar Grove Fire Chief. "He might have gone in to call for Jake."

"Who's Jake?" asked the Chief. He was worried that his crew might be looking for two men now.

"He's our family dog," Jimmy explained. He could see talking was taking its toll on his mother. "Jake didn't make it either. We didn't know he had gone back in. Mom and I ran over just as the ceiling or all of the second floor or something dropped on the kitchen and back of the house. There was a huge crash and the sparks shot out everywhere," Jimmy explained. He left out the screams.

As he and his mother arrived at the big tree out front, his father wasn't there. They watched as their home crashed in on itself. Through the crash and the sparks they heard the screams. They echoed through the night and bounced off the pastures. Mother and son looked at each other and instantly they both knew.

"No, we don't know why he went back in," Jimmy repeated.

The night of the fire changed plans. Jimmy and his father were to partner and farm their land together. Jimmy and his mother lost their partner that night. Walking in his fields the next morning, Jimmy thought.

His life and new family were before him. He decided to go on with the farming plans, but his new partner will be his young son. Jimmy had to transition from student to teacher. Jim, Sr. and son had talked for years about their partnership and how Sr. would teach Jr. Now, it was the same plan, but fast-forwarded a generation. He hoped the land and his son would be patient.

What to plant? That was easy. Cotton, corn, soybeans. When to plant? What brand and hybrid? How much fertilizer? What about weed control? What about the equipment? Was it the right tractor? Attachments? Budgets? Loans? Too many questions, and the answers were left in the charred rubble of the big house.

Cedar Grove came to the family. Some brought a dinner, all brought love. The funeral would be simple. The Pattersons had talked about what they wanted at this time, and it was simple, but no one thought it would be this soon. The plot had been decided upon several decades ago. Mr. Patterson would be buried in the family section of a cemetery close to the farm. His parents, aunts, uncles and ancestors were there. A big stone declaring PATTERSON was there too, weathering.

The funeral, burial, and tears all went by quickly, then it was over.

Jimmy realized that he was very much alone. Soon he found himself in his father's old, almost antique pick up truck, bouncing down a field road in the direction of the county road and then the county co-op. There he will find his seed and some answers. Bo and Carl Lee had been trusted by his father. Jimmy decided to continue that trust for now. There was comfort to have advisors again.

The men at the co-op knew about the fire. The entire county had heard it. They were ready with their sympathies when Jimmy pulled up and walked in. Carl Lee took the lead. "Good morning Jimmy. We are so sorry to hear about your daddy."

"Thanks guys. I have a lot of work to do. I need your help."

They talked about the planting and options. The co-op men were helpful and took their new student slow. They feared Jim, Sr. was watching, and they wanted to do right for the son.

Do right.

"Now, Jimmy you pull over to the loading dock. Bo will get you loaded right up," Carl Lee offered.

The men split off in various directions to do the work. Soon Jimmy had a truck and trailer loaded with seed and a plan scribbled on the back of a dirty co-op calendar. He knew what to do. Relief.

Farmers are religious. They have a keen sense of Who controls the weather and Nature. There are many prayers offered up from the fields.

Jimmy prayed on the blacktop as he drove back to his farm. It felt odd not to pull into the drive leading to the old house. He passed that one and turned up the drive leading to the barn and workshops. Behind him in a cloud of dust, Bo came to a stop. "Figured you need a hand to unload that seed," Was Bo's greeting.

"You are a hero," replied Jimmy. "I was wondering how to lift these bags by myself. You need to be careful. If word gets out that the co-op provides service, you'll be working hard all the time." Jimmy advised.

"Not to worry. Carl Lee isn't too keen on us getting out away from that loading dock. He will keep me close to the work there." Bo was puffing now from the exertion. His co-op cap was twisted to one side, but he still would not pass for a white rapper.

Jimmy looked closely at Bo. He appreciated the extra help. Bo's dirty cap was twisted so the bill fell over his right ear. His dark hair peeked out everywhere. He was a chewer, which also meant he was a spitter. Bo was wiry and strong. His work was punctuated with a spit directed to nothing in particular. His overalls reflected the chores he had done since the last laundry. Grease, dust and chemical stains told the story. Sometimes he quoted scripture as he worked. Otherwise he remained silent.

"Jimmy, you call on us any time you need help or have some questions. Carl Lee and I are here to help you any way we can." He was preparing to leave.

"Thank you, Bo, I'll need to call on you as I learn more about what and when I should be doing things around here. I especially need advice on herbicides." Jimmy hitched up his own coveralls as he hopped down from his truck.

Back out in his fields, about to go home, Jimmy offered a prayer of thanks for the help and advice he got at the co-op. The next day he was going to till and plant his first corn crop. The cotton and beans would come later.

Prayer.

"Katherine, where are you, honey?" Jimmy opened the door to his trailer home looking for family.

His wife appeared around the corner with her apron filled with cut flowers and Jimbo following, kicking the dirt as he walked.

Katherine was a high school beauty that kept her stunning looks into motherhood. She had long blonde hair, which usually was tied up in a ponytail when she was outside. She and Jimmy had been childhood sweethearts with a love that grew as they grew up.

Their first-born was prenamed. It went from Jim, the grandfather to Jimmy, Jr., the son, to Jim,III, now Jimbo to make it easy when calling for the men of the family. Jimmy looked at his wife and son. It was a mixed feeling of happiness and big responsibility at the same time. He smiled, and got two smiles returned for his one. A good deal any time.

Jimmy was strong. He had the athlete build and honed muscles from hard farm work. He had dark hair and blue eyes that flashed as he told jokes and teased everyone around. His sense of humor was his trademark around Cedar Grove. People liked him. He had the honesty and integrity passed down from his father. Most of his deals were done on a handshake. His word was his bond. No need for long written contracts. Jimmy had struggled for several months after his father had died figuring out his responsibilities of the farm, and his family responsibilities for his mother, wife and baby. He generally kept his sense of humor throughout, but his anchor was his faith that guided him to find his balance and his stride.

He heard his father from past plantings, "Check the tractor and equipment before you get into the field." Grunting a little to lift the hood, he checked oil and radiator fluid. All looked good, but it had been a long winter. He called the John Deere dealership. A mechanic was on his way.

"I felt it needed your expert attention before I put it to work this Spring," Jimmy told the mechanic.

"No problem. This won't take long. You'll be out there in no time." The mechanic looked like a smaller version of co-op Bo.

Jimmy was feeling more confident and less alone. He had the co-op and John Deere as advisors and supporters. Plus, he had the secret weapons he hadn't talked with yet: the boys down at Lilly's general store. He pulled his truck up to a row of pickups, and walked to the side door. Jimmy wondered why Lilly's door squeaked so loud announcing his arrival. He guessed it was a form of a security alarm. All heads turned in his direction; he nodded to the men.

Jim, Sr. made it a point to get his coffee often at the store. The coffee was awful, but he got to chat with friends. Mostly they complained about the weather, prices and politics. Jimmy had been coming along on these coffee breaks since before he could walk. These men were additional fathers for him. The men felt that way too. All were farmers. All knew they would now be teachers. Jimmy, the student, had a lot of attention focused on him. They went through Jimmy's Spring planting plan. A few adjustments were made, but only after the men in coveralls and boots finished their heated discussion. All felt a responsibility to Jim, Sr.

Do Right.

The Boys at Lilly's Store

Men, retired mostly, all across the world in cities, villages, tribes, and in Cedar Grove gather to talk. Often it is about the weather, or politics, but usually it is about what was. In them the past is still fresh, the present is unsettled, and the future uncertain. They sit on courthouse or park benches, around restaurant tables, and in the past, pot bellied stoves for warmth. At Lilly's Merle, Bobby, Clarence, Wayman, Barney and Buck have been meeting for coffee longer than any them can remember. Jim, Sr. was part of the crew until the fire and they miss him like a brother. Merle is the oldest and he tends to drift in and out of the conversations. He seems to prefer his private memories to the current affairs of the world. Each man had a history of work, hard farming like Jim Patterson. Each understood the challenges of the land. Bobby was the Postmaster so his experiences were different. He watched their struggles and delivered their mail. He brought the good and bad news to their doorsteps every day, and felt a kinship with each of them. Wayman was more of a cattleman than what he called a dirt farmer. He wore the same overalls, but he preferred a cowboy boot with the high heel compared to the other work boots of his friends. His were just as dirty so no one thought he was being "uppity." Barney and Buck tried to live into their names. Barney played the clown and brought humor to the group while Buck often tried to play the tough guy, which everyone then ignored. The combination of men and their personalities held the group together long enough to finish a cup of coffee so they repeated the ritual day after day. Sometimes

Merle didn't say a word because he was deep inside his own memories, but he also enjoyed having the company. Merle was a horse man, he didn't farm.

Jimmy was in good hands. Lilly's market was in downtown Cedar Grove, and still had Oklahoma's dust on the shelves from a few decades ago delivered by the winds of the dust bowl. Next-door was the Post Office with the flag always flying. The postmaster, Bobby, knew everyone in the area and all about their families. He was the encyclopedia and history books of Cedar Grove. Across the road was a low-slung metal building that could have been a small warehouse or storage shed. Instead it housed on one end, a pizza shop, then a beauty salon, finally at the other end was some kind of church. It didn't identify with any denomination, but did have a large sign declaring "JESUS is LORD over Cedar Grove."

Often in the parking lot was an old man selling produce out of the back of his red pick up truck. He had everything: watermelons, tomatoes, onions, and beans. He chose to let the business run itself, and he was generally gone. Most of his sales were on the honor system. He left a jar in the back of his truck between the watermelons with a price sheet under it. Customers would select what they wanted, calculate the cost, and deposit the right amount in his jar. You could see into the jar and figure how much money was sitting there, but in memory, no one had ever stolen from the old man.

Do Right.

It was efficient selling, and he forgot about taxes. It was hard to beat his produce. The only other building across the road was a combination gym and tanning place that rarely had any cars in front of it. Apparently farmers got enough sun and a work out with their daily lives.

"Momma, don't worry about me. I've got our bases covered for planting. We'll worry about the harvest later." Jimmy was telling his mother, Emily, about the help he received from the co-op, the tractor shop, and the boys down at Lilly's. His mother knew they were in good hands and all the goodwill her husband had banked was now paying dividends back to his family. Emily smiled at her son and gave a quick prayer of thanks. She missed her husband.

Intermixed with the goodwill was an ill wind blowing from the neighboring farm. The wind had a name: Bud. He enjoyed run-ins with everyone including Jim, Sr. Now his target was Jim, Jr. He wanted the Patterson land. His hope was that Jimmy would fail at farming and sell the land for a song. Bud thought he would help Jimmy---fail.

Jimmy was out plowing the next morning. It was a cool part of the day with the sun low on the horizon and a mist rising over the woods in the distance. He could inhale the air like it was a substance needed for his soul. The fresh turned soil had its own smell. It was dark and ready from the long winter. Nutrients were soon to flow into the cotton seeds and start the cycle on the land yet again. He was excited as the sun began to warm the soil and him.

Jimmy saw the movement as he made a wide turn of the tractor to make another perfectly straight row. The diesel of the John Deere rumbled smoothly even with the strain of plowing on it. He rolled to a stop, turned everything to idle, and hopped to the freshly plowed ground.

There he saw movement again. This time it was between his boots. He picked up the fur ball of a puppy and headed home.

"Jimbo, look what I found." Jimmy hollered up the drive. Bursting from the trailer with a full-grown black lab came the curious son. The abandoned puppy transferred from father to son. The lab was as curious as the boy. The puppy got sniffed. The boy could not understand why anyone would toss out a perfectly good puppy in the country. The father shook his head at the image of city people throwing away their responsibility to country folk who would raise and train this puppy.

A good farm dog is a valuable asset. The dog becomes a part of the farming process, but mainly is good company in a lonesome business. Most dogs hear the ideas and options of intricate farm plans. A good dog will keep his ears up as his master talks through a problem and once in a while will wag his tail in agreement to a decision. Many a farmer makes a final decision based upon a wag of a tail. Jim Sr.'s dog, Jake, had been the best of a long string of farm dogs on the land. Often the grandfather would consult with the co-op and the boys down at Lilly's but make the final decision after Jake chose to wag his tail. That dog had a good track record. That could have been going through the grandfather's mind when he went back into his blazing house. Jimmy and his mother felt the loss of the two souls.

"Time for me to get back to plowing. You and mom should name this new pup." With that, he turned walking back to his green and yellow tractor still sitting in the field.

There is a farmer's pride in plowing straight rows, then planting straight. Everything had to be straight or the boys down at Lilly's would talk about you. Jimmy knew they would drive by sometime to inspect his rows. They looked straight to him.

After the first rainstorm, they learned that their new puppy was afraid of thunder.

Burton

Little boys and puppies grow fast. The puppy got his name: Hank. He grew to be a pretty lab and golden retriever mix. He grew more fearful of storms too. When thunder rumbled, Hank would bolt in any direction and blindly run away with the older lab following. One particularly bad storm they ran, but didn't return home for two weeks. The phone rang.

"Mister, are you missing two dogs?" asked a voice very distinctly Southern country.

The two men chatted for a minute, and directions were given. Jimmy backed his truck away from his home and followed the directions to a cluster of mobile homes scattered in random angles. Sitting on the porch of one was a pretty young girl with an older man. Each held a leash, which held the old lab and Hank. Jimmy got out of his truck. Introductions were made. The girl and her father had found the wayward dogs, and had been feeding them. The tags gave them Jimmy's phone number. The dogs hopped in the back of Jimmy's truck. They panted their happiness. The girl, in her early teens was very pretty, and used her Southern manners with a lot of "sirs" expressed. Her father resembled a character from the movie, Deliverance. Jimmy listened for banjo music, and was relieved when he didn't hear any. The two men faced each other, talking. The man went by the name of Burton. He was a Johnson, one of the early settler families of the area.

His eyes didn't focus. One looked straight ahead, the other looked off sharply to the left. It was difficult talking. Jimmy didn't know which eye to talk to. Burton's coveralls had seen a lot of work, grease and dirt, but rarely a washing machine. His camouflaged hat was dirtier than the clothes. Burton smelled.

Burton's straight eye looked at Jimmy while his other one was occupied by activity over Jimmy's left shoulder. Soon Burton shouted,

"Hey there. Stop that, damn it!"

Jimmy thought Burton was shouting at him since he was talking to the one straight eye. Burton passed by Jimmy picking up speed. Jimmy turned around to his left as he saw a dog fly through the air from Burton's boot. Three other hounds, a pit bull mix, a Rottweiler mix, and a Sheppard mix were pulling a cat in several different directions. There was squalling.

In almost a whisper the little girl said, "That's my cat."

"I'm so sorry. I hope it is OK," replied Jimmy.

In a much louder voice she said "It's da-aid!"

"Oh no, that's awful," he said.

"It's alright. It happens quite of-ten." She said matter-of-factly.

Then the little girl turned and shouted, "Daddy, I'm going to Grandmama's."

She trotted over to another trailer that barely squatted on the big cinder block bricks trying to keep it level. Behind her more dogs were flying through the air as the lifeless cat lay where the dogs had left it. Jimmy thought it best to go home with his found dogs. He paused while he thought this time he did hear banjo music playing in the background.

Jimbo was excited to get Hank back. After Katherine heard the story, she began to check the dogs for ticks and fleas.

The next day was cool with the promise of heat later. The American flag in the yard was hanging down indicating no wind. God's day was beginning. Jimmy turned the orange key in his green and yellow tractor and heard the diesel roar to life. He let it idle to warm up before he asked it to do any heavy work. Today he was going to plant his first crop. The soil had been tilled. The rows were straight. He calibrated the attached planter according to the co-op's instructions for corn. All systems were a "go." Jimmy said the first of many prayers for the day.

Prayer.

He turned towards the fresh black soil warming in

the Spring sun, turning a few knobs, watching his speed, he began the planting. He drove straight. Prayers for rain. More prayers for warm temperatures. More prayers for minimal pests and weeds. Prayers for his family.

A few weeks later, the green tops of the corn stalks began to appear. From a distance it looked like a green fuzz on the earth. Up close the big, strong sprigs of corn stalk looked like answered prayers.

That evening with the sun almost down, Jimmy turned his tractor up the lane to where dinner was being prepared. Jimbo, Hank, the lab, and some unknown man waited for him at the end of the lane.

The outstretched hand had this attached: "Hi, I'm Billy Berkley, I ain't raight."

"Hello, I'm Jimmy Patterson. Glad to meet you."

Billy then related how he had fallen off construction scaffolding some time ago and fell on his head.

"I ain't been raight since," he declared. "I came by to congratulate you on your new crop and to invite you to our church just down the road in Cedar Grove."

Billy wore traditional coveralls and an explorer type pith helmet/hat that looked lost from a jungle exploration. A chinstrap kept it level. He mowed the lawn and trimmed the bushes at his church, and was proud of his work. Billy was actually quite bright before his accident, and he tended to keep to himself and preferred to think about things. He also was an avid photographer, and read his Bible. He was long every-where. His face was long, his arms hung low, he was tall with a long, almost pointed nose. His eyes were a dark brown that gave him a sort of intellectual look if he made eye contact with you, which was rare. His hands were like a farmers' work hands. They were rough, hard, and long bony fingers, they looked like tree roots. Billy would rub his index finger against his thumb as he talked to help the words come out.

"Thank you for the invitation, but we belong to a little church over at Spring Creek."

They talked about crops, churches and the need to secure scaffolding as the sun went down. Billy declined a dinner invitation, but did tell Katherine that he raised chickens and he would sell her eggs direct at 50 cents less than what she pays at Lilly's. Only thing is she would have to drive about an hour deeper into the country. Lilly's looked like a bargain price, but then again, Billy ain't right.

Dinner. A long, hot shower. Stories for Jimbo, then bed for Jimmy. It had been a long, dusty day for him. He needed sleep.

Buzzards. That is the first sign of a dead cow. Jimmy hadn't planned a detour to the cow pastures this morn-ing, but the circling buzzards made him change the plans for the day. Plowing would commence after he disposed of the carcass. $1,000+ dollars lost.

"Well, the birds will be well fed," he muttered. He knew he would have to gather the bones and carcass later, which was an unpleasant job.

What he didn't know was that the ill wind/Bud last night had sighted his deer rifle to a point right behind the shoulder blade of the cow, squeezed the trigger, felt the recoil, and smiled.

The phone was ringing a few mornings later. Mumbling, Jimmy said. "Hello."

"Your cows are out in the road." Came from the other end of the line.

Jimmy quickly got dressed, drove to his pasture, rounded up the few wayward cows, and then walked the fence line to find the opening. Cut. Someone had cut his barbed wire fence. The ends were even, sharply cut, and were shiny. Bud came immediately to mind. Another worry on top of worries.

The Patterson cowherd had started two generations ago with three good Angus/Hereford mix cows and a fine pure Angus bull. The calves reflected the mix and often had white faces leading people to call them black baldies. The Hereford strain made good mothers and easier birthing, the Angus added quick weight gain and general good health. The Pattersons had a top quality herd, which supported their families.

"Jimbo, the donkey is in the cowherd for a reason," Father attempting to answer another series of questions.

"When the cow gives birth, it attracts coyotes, which will then try to eat the baby." continued the father as the eyes widened on the son. "Our donkey there bonds with the cowherd, he feels responsible. He also doesn't like coyotes and is not afraid of them. If a coyote or several show up, our friend here will lay back his long ears, charge at them, and chase them away from the defenseless calf."

"Instead of a guard dog, we have a guard donkey," concluded Jimbo.

Since the fire, Jimmy had planted the corn, prepared the soil for cotton, then beans, serviced all the equipment, watched over new calves joining the herd. He and the farm were on a roll. The weather was cooperating, the boys down at Lilly's were advising. All was good except he kept worrying and feeling the presence of the ill wind.

"Jimmy you should ignore Bud," Katherine advised.

"Yes, I know Kate, but he has gone from passive annoyance to active aggression." Jimmy responded.

"Now you don't know that he is the one killing our cows and cutting our fences, it might be random kids with no sense," she offered. "Jimmy, you don't have any proof that Bud did these things, we need to just keep going, and not get distracted."

"You are probably right, but I want to make him stop or find a way to get him arrested," Jimmy was mad.

He shared his anger with the Lilly's boys, which prompted each to tell a "Bud story." There was little goodwill that Bud had built up over the years.

Once he sold a lot to some city people, got in an argument, and then put up a no trespassing sign on the only road leading to the lot. Another time he had an 80-year-old grandmother and her grandsons arrested for mowing over an unmarked property line on a cemetery they maintained as volunteers for the community. He also seemed to argue with everyone who owned land next to his. He wanted to push his line into his neighbors' property. Lately his focus was on the Patterson farm, and how he could get the land.

Most people didn't like him. He was short, stocky, and had close cropped graying hair. He looked a bit like a bulldog seeking trouble. His sneer kept away friendly conversation. His eyes told the truth that he wasn't all that bright. He was mean-spirited, and Jimmy was learning that now. "Son, people like Bud usually get what's coming to them. Keep your mind and energy focused on your work and farm." Advised the friendly, good ol' boys down at Lilly's.

Billy Berkley stopped in to get some coffee one morning.

"Billy, what do you think about a guy like Bud?" one of the farmers, Clarence, asked as he poured himself some more bad coffee. Billy was a frequent loiterer at

Lilly's usually as a listener, and rarely contributed to the conversation.

"I think a man must first have peace within himself. If not, then he will spread that inner conflict to innocents outside of himself and contaminate the air with his anger. Families, clans, countries should do the same to stop wars," Billy quietly replied. Merle was closed within himself and paid no attention.

Father and son were singing country songs in the cab checking on the corn. Jimmy drove down the lane past the woods where he hunts deer in the Fall and turkey in the Spring, past the large pond where he and his father loved to fish bass and the flat bluegill. On his left are the fields and on his right are the woods and he can see down into the hollows of the woods and remember the explorations of his youth. He hopes his son has the same experiences as he grows up on this land.

Thunder soon mixed with the singing. Jimmy thought about Hank hoping he was in the house. With pride he looked over the tall, straight, green rows of his cornfield. The next morning after the storm, the tall corn was laid low. A straight-line wind funneled between two small hills focused the power of the wind so that it blew the cornstalks to the point of breaking.

His tall field now was reduced to stalks about two

feet high. Corn husks were on the ground, soon to rot. The first corn crop was a bust. There would be no harvest this year. Jimmy sought comfort down at Lilly's. Then he planned to take his wife to dinner.

As the sun rose, Father and son hopped down from the tractor and began walking through what was left of a once beautiful cornfield. After a short walk into the remaining tall, good corn, the stalks were up to Jimmy's shoulders and covering up Jimbo. All he could see at his short level was green. Father and son held hands.

"Daddy why did God do this?" Jimbo wanted to know.

Jimmy got down to his son's level. Both were covered by green.

"Son, there are often reasons we don't understand, but you still have to trust in Him."

"But where is God?" the questions continued.

"Jimbo, He is every where and all around us. It is like us here in this field asking, "Where is the corn? As you know, it is all around us, and everywhere. God is in everything we see and is with us all the time. I take comfort knowing He is with me in all I do. I think there is only one Truth in our world, and that is that God loves us. As you grow up, and realize how hard life can be at times, you will realize how important that one Truth is. Especially when you feel all alone."

Prayer.

"Kate, it's a mess. I worry about the money we were going to get from that crop. Now we have to depend on the other crops and the herd. This is going to be a skimpy year." Jimmy felt failure.

"We will have the herd and the other crops, think about that and let the corn go. We don't have to start building our house this year anyway. We can wait a year," she replied. Both had been dreaming of building a real house and getting out of the trailer. A new house could give the room needed for a new child. They had dreams that were blown away by the wind.

Sitting at a quiet corner table, Jimmy and Kate made a handsome couple. He was a former high school and college athlete. She was a former cheerleader. He was getting weathered, and had the classic "farmer's tan." He was strong as a young man, and was solid as a rock now. She was softened by motherhood, but retained that youthful glow. Together they could move mountains, raise a family, farm.

"Honey, I want to bring Jimbo along with me daily to the fields," He said.

"I worry about his safety. He is pretty active even though he is about ten now, and that machinery is dangerous," she replied.

"I'll watch him. He needs to learn," That ended the issue. Jimbo was to become a partner in the family business. A farmer.

"Turn the key to the right." The small fingers did, and the massive machine rumbled to life. Jimbo shuddered. He and his dad were going to work. With the father's one hand on the wheel, the son turned the John Deere to face the fields. Father worked the pedals, son thought he was steering alone. It was snug in the cab. They shared body heat in the cool of the morning. Jimmy explained the various controls, knobs and gauges. Jimbo thought he must be in a rocket ship. Heading to cotton fields rather than the moon, both smiled. Jimmy told stories of farming accidents and how it was important to be safe around the tractor and attachments. The machinery had hurt too many hard working people. Lessons from the grandfather were passing through the son to the grandson. Generational advice.

"Son we can't stop every five minutes for you to pee or this cotton will never get planted."

"Dad, it is important this time. I really, really need to go, NOW."

The noise of the green and yellow beast grew softer, then stopped. The rumble continued in their heads. Jimbo hopped down, did his business, crawled back up into the cab. Morning cool was turning to afternoon hot. Sweat formed. Air conditioning came on in the cab. Father and son worked the straight rows as the sun lowered, and finally went out. The remaining rows were planted by the headlights. Jimbo slept.

Some prayers were answered. The weather brought rain when needed, the co-op men were right on track with herbicides and pesticides. Cotton grew. Father and son walked the rows, checking for bugs.

"Boweevils can ruin a crop my daddy told me, so check early and check often." Jimmy passed along more advice hoping his son would retain some of it.

Jimbo heard the words, but his mind drifted. He was thinking that he was walking in snow. From a distance, ripe cotton looks like snow on a field. Jimbo pretended he was cold walking in snowdrifts. In fact, it was hot and humid. Heat waves were sweltering up from the ground. The blue sky hurt his eyes, it was so bright. Sweat was forming. No frost here.

Jimbo watched as the John Deere men put a gigantic attachment on the front of his familiar tractor.

"That's a cotton picker there, son," said one mechanic with the familiar green and yellow cap.

"A picker is one of the most dangerous pieces of equipment on a farm, advised the partner mechanic with the same type cap. Lots of good folks have been hurt real bad by one of these things."

Jimbo took a step back from the monster.

"See, brush gets tangled in these picking teeth. If you get in a hurry, don't turn everything off, and try to clear out the brush, then it will grab you and pull you into the picker. Some people lose hands, arms and their lives by such accidents. Always turn the tractor off before touching anything near here," advised the man.

More scary stories and advice were offered by the guys in Carhart overalls and John Deere caps. Jimbo thought of the bright white cotton splattered with bright red blood. He decided to keep away from the picking teeth that would pull him into the beast.

The weather held. No rain. Fields dry. Time to pick cotton. Father and son were tired from long days. The John Deere tractor kept up its steady roar and steady picking day and night. The cotton was off the plants, picked, loaded in a contraption that squeezed it into a tight brick the size of an 18 wheeler truck trailer, then a tarp was snugged over the cotton brick in case of rain. Eventually the cotton gin people came to haul the bricks to the gin. Cotton left, money returned. The boys down at Lilly's still complained about prices, but cotton prices these days were pretty decent. Jimmy spent the first cotton dollars on another dinner with his wife.

"Our next challenge is the beans," he told her.

"Soybeans are pretty sensitive. That soybean rust continues to invade counties in Tennessee up from Mississippi, so we have to spray for that. The weed spraying is particularly important. The guys at the co-op will have to guide me there so I don't kill the beans along with the weeds." Jimmy learned to farm and worry from his father.

"Jimmy, you are looking for trouble. Relax, and let's celebrate success in cotton. Your beans will be fine, and we still have the cows," his sensible wife said as the plates were being served.

A night out was special for the two of them. Money was tight from the loss of the corn crop. They still had their new house to dream and save for too.

While Jimmy was learning to relax and enjoy his dinner, the ill wind was kicking up. Bud was mixing chemicals in his work shed. The concoction was a weed killer, but he mixed it extra strong. This stuff was so concentrated it could kill a tree. Most farmers don't spray with a strong wind blowing.

Bud waited until the wind was blowing in the direction of Jimmy's bean crop. The next day he sprayed, the chemicals drifted to Jimmy's land and beans. It took about 24 hours for the soybeans to turn brown and die. The boys down at Lilly's added another chapter to Bud stories. Bud was breaking the sacred trust farmers have for one another.

"Katherine, part of the beans are lost, the bills have come in, the bank people might show up any day now." Jimmy was discouraged.

It was hard enough to battle Nature, but add a malicious neighbor, and it was an unfair fight. Katherine kept up her encouragement, but now she was getting scared. Jimmy and Katherine took Jimbo with them to visit the rock of the family, Jimmy's mother, Emily. They told her about the corn loss, some shot cows, the cut fences, and the chemical killing of the bean crop. Emily's eyes narrowed as she followed the tale. She looked up, prayed for strength and wisdom, and imagined what her husband would do.

"Jimmy, you go over and confront Bud, tell him to leave this land and this family alone." Emily's softness to the world hardened that night.

"Jimmy we have no proof that Bud did anything. Confronting him might just make him meaner. I also think you should take the Sheriff with you," Katherine was trying to be a voice of reason.

Before Jimmy could call the Sheriff, the law knocked on his door. Next to the Sheriff was Billy Berkley with his digital camera, grinning like a beaver. Billy had photos of Bud spraying chemicals as the wind blew towards Jimmy's crop. He also had a photo of Bud taking aim at one of the Patterson's cows. No mistake about it. Then there was the photo of Bud cutting Jimmy's fence. The Sheriff went to make an arrest; Billy went to trim the churchyard. Jimmy and Katherine went out to measure where their new house would sit. Billy had few interests beyond mowing and praying. One was photography and he had collected a fine camera and lenses that he could photograph from a distance and in low light and, even in the dark with infrared attachments. He liked everyone, but shared the community dislike for Bud and followed him on the few times when Bud did the mischief against the Pattersons. His photos were always in focus. The Sheriff was convinced and made the arrest. Bud's assault on the Pattersons was over.

The ill wind stopped at once. Jimmy sold off part of the cowherd.

All except the area where Bud's chemicals killed a portion of Jimmy's soybean crop, yields were outstanding.

The harvest was completed in dry weather. Money reversed the direction flow. It was coming in, instead of going out. Jimmy could feel the vibrancy of his land.

Mother Earth.

He turned up the country music in the cab of his tractor, He and Jimbo sang along.

The Pattersons held a family meeting. The season was over. What money was to come in was in. Expenses were paid. The family discussed, and then decided that, if a new house was to be built, then it would first be for Emily, the grandmother. Jimmy and Katherine would wait for next year. The decision was supported by a wag of the tail from Hank, so all knew the right one had been made. The family funds were combined.

Emily was to get her new house. With another wag of the tail, a new porch swing was added.

Emily had been living in an old house on the land where a farm manager once lived so she was more than ready to move out of the small quarters and into a larger house.

"Jimbo, as we walk the fields, think about the land." Father and son stretching their legs from another long day in the tractor cab. "The land is what sustains our family. You must always respect it. You and I are temporary stewards of God's land.

Mother Earth.

We must care for it and think about any long-term affects we might do. We shouldn't abuse it for short-term gain. Our role is to *do things right*. We don't over plant and ruin the topsoil, we don't over use chemicals, which can hurt the soil and run off and get into the streams, which can harm the fish, frogs and wildlife. As they were talking, a sound like a traffic jam of honking horns came from over head. Looking up father and son saw a V shape flock of Canadian Geese migrating South. Another link in Nature and a part of country living.

You and I have a responsibility to the land and all the critters that rely on it to live. Our family relies on it too, year after year." Jimbo put on his serious face and listened.

"Daddy, did grandpa take care of this land too?"

"Of course he did. He passed it down to us in good shape."

"We will care for it too, and then you can pass it down to your children."

"But I don't like girls. Can I have kids without the bother of a wife?"

"Son, that is a discussion for another day. We'll talk about the birds and the bees later," said the father.

"But I don't like bees either." The son was not going with the flow, but the father hoped that some of the land discussion would stick. A new season was about to begin,

It was dry. A good time to put equipment in the field. They planted the corn first. No rain, so they used the time to plant the cotton, then the beans. Rainfall was half of normal with none in the fore-cast. Seeds can't germinate and grow without water. Jimmy worried like generations of Pattersons had done in the past. He took his worries to Lilly's.

"Hi guys, sure is dry out there," Jimmy said as the door squeaked his arrival.

The Lilly's boys then commenced to argue over memories of past dry times.

"It was drier in '42. That year most farmers just gave up."

"Barney you can't remember that, you weren't even here in '42. You were off fighting in Italy then."

"I got letters from home, Buck, and don't forget that I am a trained killer. The US government trained me to kill, then sent me overseas."

Barney was trying to look tough, but that is hard to do with tobacco stains on your chin mixed with the mustard from his hot dog. All agreed it was dry and would be a hard year for everyone. Bankers were nervous.

A few hours later Jimmy watched from his truck as Jimbo chased Hank around the trailer home. Little puffs of dust came from where feet trotted. "We need rain," prayed Jimmy. His throat was as parched as the land. Well water is the best when you are thirsty. Jimmy worried if it was possible for his well to run dry. The land was hurting.

Mother Earth.

Cracks due to the dryness formed in all the fields, Trees began to wilt early. The land looked sad, desperate. Grass stopped growing, turned brown. Cows would soon get hungry.

"Boys, Do you know where I can buy some hay?" Jimmy sought advice and comfort at the general store.

All looked at each other. Finally, Clarence cleared his throat.

"Jimmy, we are all in the same boat. There's no grass growing, no hay to be bought. You can't even go to the sale barn with your herd. Too many have already gone there and prices are rock bottom. Best thing to do is rotate them from pasture to pasture until it rains."

"I don't wish ill for other folks, but a good hurricane down in the gulf would help us get a couple of days rain up here," Clarence was looking for a bright side to nature. Merle looked up but didn't say anything; he adjusted his weight and went back to his memories.

Merle

He wears the uniform. His was denim overalls and brown leather work boots. He wears a baseball type cap that advertises a trucking company. Everything was clean but everything was very worn and had stories to tell. Merle was the oldest of the group at 93, born in 1897. When the earth turned and the clock struck 1900, he celebrated being potty trained. This was before, "You Da Man," high fives, fist bumps and thumbs ups. All he got were smiles and a few rubs on his head, but he knew everyone was proud of him. His memory goes back that far. He plays his memory like a tape player rewinding in time. He can skip some parts, but some insist he revisit and feel the pain again. Sometimes he gets to feel the joy. Merle came to Cedar Grove as a young boy with his family about 1912. His extended family included uncles and others that swore they remembered stories from "THE War." That would be the Civil War or the Yankee Aggression or other names depending on your location around the Mason-Dixon line. One uncle recounted how his father was walking around Jackson, TN just 30 miles down the road from Cedar Grove, when he ran into Gen. US Grant and his staff strolling in downtown Jackson on the way back to his house on East Main Street by the railroad. The Yankees had taken Jackson, and Grant was using it as a headquarters after the big Battle of Shiloh. He commandeered a nice house on Main Street in which to live. Confederate General Nathan Bedford Forrest was using his forces to disrupt the railroad supplies that Grant wanted for his Mississippi campaign and pester Grant's forces. Merle, as a boy, got to hear the stories first hand from his relatives. He could hear his uncle's voice rise with emotion as he told about the fighting boys in gray protecting the land from the invaders in blue. His hands would twitch sometimes as if he were pulling triggers on guns or ropes on cannon. His eyes would fade out of the present and go into the past to listen to his uncle.

Merle was basically a horseman. His long frame

was still erect like he was riding a horse. He disliked motorized vehicles and wore the trucking cap as a mocking device and humor known only to himself. He was still very strong for his age. When he was younger, he was very strong. His arms today still could turn a headstrong horse, but his hands were gentle. He could tickle the reins, which would jiggle the bit in the horse's mouth and control it without pain. His hands were like cords of steel or like tree roots. Strong, responsive only to his will. Gentle if he willed it or crushing if the situation called for it. His memory replayed the times he gently made love to his wife with those hands and the times he had to kill with the same hands. He moaned a bit in the memories.

"Merle, you all right old man?" Bobbie asked as he poured him a fresh cup of coffee. It took a moment for the fog to clear and the past to move to the present.

"Thank you, I'm fine. More coffee is just what I needed, " he replied.

For a while Merle tried hard to stay in the present and be part of the talk about the crops and the weather, but the past was pulling him and his attention back.

Merle could taste the mud. The sound was deafening, more than all the fourth of Julys combined. He was cold. Merle looked to his right and saw his buddy with his helmet askew and fear in his eyes. His gun was at his side, limp, so Merle helped him set it up straight because they were going to have to charge to the next row, ditch, ravine, trench. There it came. The command, the trumpet blare, again. Young men leapt out of one safe trench and charged into bullets to take control of the next trench and a few more yards of the battlefield. Merle could run, and he did. He fired his gun as he ran at the little bursts of light coming from the trench he was running towards. His buddy on his right fell from a bullet to the chest. Merle picked him up with one arm and kept running. He was ahead of most and vulnerable to the bullets whizzing everywhere around his head. He dove into the trench and propped up his dying buddy. A German soldier attacked with a bayonet attached to the end of his rifle. Merle dodged that, grabbed the rifle barrel and the soldier's throat almost at the same time. He squeezed the life out of the soldier who dropped the rifle as he gasped for air. Both the enemy and his buddy died in that trench at about the same time. Part of him died that day too. He wasn't 20 yet, and WW1 was raging across Europe. He remembered the mud, and the running, and the fear. He tried to fast forward past the war to when he came home to Sarah, but his mind wouldn't let him off easy. He had to go through all the war again, and the pain. Sarah knew him and yet she didn't know him. She knew him before the war, but didn't know who came back. Since the beginning of time man knows war is awful and it does terrible things to those who survive it. Since the Civil War we have tried to put a name on "it." We call it Soldier's Heart, Shell Shock, Battle Fatigue, and recently, Post Traumatic Stress Disorder (PTSD). Merle called it being screwed up and "out of sorts." Sarah called it "hurt." Whatever it was, it created a distance between them. He wouldn't or couldn't talk about what bothered him. He preferred the company of horses to that of people. They sensed and seemed to know his hurt. He could communicate with them and not with her. She withdrew too so a gulf between them grew. He spent his days, then the nights at the barn. Their marriage grew cold until you couldn't call it a marriage anymore. She would watch him, sometimes; ride down the lane, erect, on his horse. He rode with the easiness of experience and confidence, the reins loose in his hands, but he was as alert as the horse to anything on the trail. Both felt like they were prey animals with a predator around every bend or rock. Merle was aware of the pain he was causing Sarah, but he couldn't do anything about it and she wasn't skilled enough, like a horse, to help him. So they existed like that until she left.

Merle stood up, unsteady at first as he drifted from the past into the present. His eyes adjusted to reality as the fog lifted. Bobby looked at him carefully. Barney and Buck continued to ignore him. Merle found his balance like you do on a new horse and walked slowly outside into the sunlight. It was almost too bright for him, but the warmth was good for his bones. He stood for a long while looking across the road at the sign declaring "Jesus is Lord over Cedar Grove." Then a tractor rumbled by spewing black diesel smoke followed by an 18-wheeler doing the same. He grunted in disgust wishing for the days of mules and wagons, turned and went back into the store to be with the boys. The boys were still talking about the drought and Jimmy was still concerned about his options.

What the ill wind: Bud, couldn't do, Nature was about to, and that was to force the Pattersons off the land.

"Kate, I'm worried."

"You always worry," replied his wife.

"The crops are just sitting there. We might not have anything to harvest unless it rains. The cows are hungry with nothing to feed them and no place to go to sell them. Creditors are calling. Without rain, we run out of options." Jimmy was worrying in high gear now.

The land was parched. Small lakes were dry with weeds popping up. Gardens were as dry as the fields. No vegetables meant more expensive trips to the grocery store. Cash had dried up at about the same rate as the land. The pastures were brown and no new grass growing, trees were wilting looking like an early fall too many months ahead of normal, the seeds in the ground could rot before they germinated wasting the time, cost, and fuel it took to put them there. The drought was throughout the country with all farmers and ranchers suffering. Creditors were nervous. Those that had any money in savings were buying up land for a song. Everyone watched the weather as more dryness was forecasted.

Hank barked, then there was a knock on the door. Jimmy opened the front door to see Bud on the porch.

"I would like to make you an offer on your farm," is what Jimmy heard. The offer was as short as the discussion.

Jimmy held Kate especially close that night feeling the pressure of 6 generations to do well and keep the land. For the first time in his life, Jimmy felt desperate. Jimbo felt the stress in the house and cried.

"Shush, listen," Kate whispered.

The boys quieted and strained to hear. Faintly, but distinctly a random ping could be heard on the roof of their mobile home. The pings increased in number and frequency. It was raining.

The family, including Hank ran outside. There was

no thunder so Hank was relaxed. All stood in the rain, looking up. Jimbo had his mouth open to catch the drops. Mom and Dad sent prayers of thanks up.

Prayer.

Hank liked the coolness of the rain on him. Life was good again. It rained all night. There was a hurricane in the Gulf pushing rain up to Tennessee. It rained for two days. The land responded immediately. Grass grew, the seeds in the ground stirred to germinate.

There would be a harvest this year. The trees were stressed as much as Jimmy, but the rain turned the leaves back to green. Cracks in the fields turned to mud. Jimmy prayed appreciation some more. The drought was over. Bankers and other creditors were relieved. Bud quit thinking of a quick buy of the Patterson land. The earth turned back to vibrancy.

Mother Earth.

Jimmy, for the first time, eased up some on the worrying.

Emily

When the smoke cleared after the tragic fire, the day was bright, but Emily's day was still hazy. Her future was uncertain, she always had Jim beside her to face all the uncertain futures of her life. She felt very much alone, and with the Patterson trait for worrying, she worried about her son and the massive job he was undertaking. She watched, and worried as he planted crops, as he dealt with the ill wind/Bud, as he dealt with the drought. Surpassing her worry was pride. Her son was doing well. Her husband would be very proud of their son.

Her face could be the billboard for a loving matriarch. She had soft eyes, which sparkled with the quick laugh. Jimbo learned what unconditional love was. Emily's hair was grayer than a mix, but not quite white. You could tell that, in her time, she was a beauty. In spite of her pretty softness, Emily was the rock of the family. Her common sense kept the Patterson worry trait in check and the family balanced in tough times. Families all over Cedar Grove often came to her for advice. Young mothers especially depended on her guidance in child rearing matters. The Baptist church looked to her for leadership on the big decisions. Miss Emily took it all in good humored stride. Her husband was a leader on the farming side, and she was a leader on the domestic side. They were a power couple of their generation.

The Baptist church mobilized after the fire. One of their flock, Emily, needed them. Food came from every direction. The pastor visited so often that Hank didn't bark anymore at him. The congregation prayed for her. She felt the embrace and was comforted by the efforts of many for the one. In her loneliness, Emily found her Bible and read it, yet again. This time she read it slower and found more meaning in it. Eventually she knew she would be fine.

Prayer.

Time from the fire, time from the death was healing. Emily began to look towards the future. Her daughter-in-law, Katherine, had a town job to help ends meet. Emily believed her role to help the family was to cook the meals. Jimmy and Jimbo enjoyed large noon dinners, as is a Southern farm custom. The evening suppers were not as large, but always good.

"Momma, your cooking is mighty fine tonight," Jimmy was showing his appreciation.

"Yes, and it is such a help to me while I have this job," Katherine was adding to the praise.

"Your meals are yummy," is what Jimbo decided to offer. Family helped Emily fill the big void in her heart and in her day.

Emily was used to being the partner in the farm business. Jim relied on her as he discussed options during each season. Jimmy found a willing ear as he often consulted his mother. The farm was thriving, and so was Emily's garden. Her good cooking was enhanced by fresh vegetables straight out of the garden. Life was looking brighter every day. The Baptist church wasn't ready to let her go. Friends included her at dinners, school events, and some of the ladies rotated as to who would pick her up and drive her to church services. Emily could not fall. There were too many hands holding her up.

"Jimbo, leave Hank alone for a minute and listen." The grandmother was seeking the grandson's attention. "You need to read more. You watch too much television and spend too much time playing those video games. You'll learn more from books. "When I was your age we didn't have television or computer games," she added.

"What? You didn't have TV? Jimbo was incredulous. What did you do then?" He couldn't imagine a day without TV and games.

"I read books," Was the quick reply. "I read the Bible and a book of poems by Emily Dickinson. She wrote a lot about nature. I appreciated her writing, replied the older woman. In fact, I don't think anyone is writing about nature anymore. Dickinson and Henry David Thoreau were great nature writers. Now there seems to be so much science fiction in bookstores, like your computer games. Well the Bible is still there." She took comfort in that fact. Grandmother and grandson were forming a special bond.

Jimbo's mind was drifting to school earlier that day when several city boys were taunting him. The taunts escalated to them pushing and shoving then hitting him. He crouched low and charged like a bull in the pasture. He hit three of them square and they fell fast. With fists clenched he turned on the other two who lifted their hands in surrender and walked away. Jimbo was strong from his daily farm work and the city boys were no match for him. He went to his classroom, angry, then home to his grandmother.

Splash, a rock hit the water in the small pond with two generations watching the ripples move from the center of the pond to the shore where they were standing.

"See Jimbo, that splash and ripples is just what happens when you do something. Your actions ripple out to affect us all. Good or bad. You must be mindful of what you are doing and how it might impact the family," advised the old woman. "We count on each other to create good ripples by telling the truth, treating other people by the Golden Rule, and doing right."

Do Right.

Emily was boring in to pre-empt bad teenage behavior.

"I understand, Grandma," Jimbo was paying attention and promising himself to be a good boy and send out only good ripples.

She took the boy's hand and began to walk. His hand, young with the promise of calloused strength, mingled with the wrinkled and old hand being led to the cemetery up a small hill from the pond. They stopped at a row of headstones with the name "Patterson" on them. The years went back to the late 1880's. The day was warm, but not hot and humid. It was pleasant for a walk. A breeze floated above the hills to comfort them and they could smell the woods nearby.

"Who you are today goes back to all these people. They lived on this land, made families, eventually died and buried back on this land. These people before us created the fine reputation and good Patterson name. It is our responsibility to live our lives worthy of those who came before us. Those pond ripples also ripple back into history. You and I should make these ancestors proud of us," Grandmother Emily was using the weight of history to impress the young boy.

"Yes ma'am," was Jimbo's only response, but he knew that he had to live up to history and his grandmother's expectations.

Do Right.

As they turned to leave they noticed a young girl placing flowers at a grave marked: Mattie. "Hello, what's your name?" asked Jimbo.

"I'm Caroline and I live in town, but I come out here often with flowers for my aunt and to spend time with her," replied the girl.

Jimbo and Caroline talked on for a while about

TOM REED

schools, family and the difference between city and country living. Finally Emily came over.

"Jimbo, it has been a long afternoon. Let's you and me go down to Lilly's market and get a cool drink,"

"Yes, ma'am I'm thirsty," it was a quick reply.

"Young lady, would you like to join us?"

"No, ma'am I have to get going back to town. My mother must be on her way to pick me up, maybe next time."

"Good-bye Caroline." He took a second look at this new and pretty girl he had never seen before.

The door squeaked their arrival. The men stood out of respect for Jimbo's grandmother. Each one offered her his chair.

"Thank you, gentlemen, but I think I'll just stand here and hold on to this boy's hand so he won't go looking for candy." Said the old woman.

"Jimbo, how about an RC cola and a moon pie," offered Clarence.

"Yes sir that is just what I've been thinking about on our walk down here." The boy let loose a smile.

The door squeaked the arrival of an old black man. He wore the typical overalls and boots. He held an old beat up cap that he nervously turned in circles in his hands.

"Can someone please tell me where Old Hickory Flat Road is?" the stranger asked.

"Yes, just keep going down this road another couple of miles and it is a gravel road on your right," replied Buck.

Jimbo quickly looked up at his grandmother. She gently squeezed his hand, which he interpreted to command, "be quiet." The black man left as the door squeaked his departure. His ancient truck sputtered to a smoky life and the man drove towards Buck's instructions, but in fact, the opposite direction from Old Hickory Flat Road. Some of the boys were racists.

Walking home with his RC cola in one hand and a wrinkled hand in his other, Jimbo wanted answers.

"Why did Mr. Buck tell that man to go in the wrong direction?"

"Jimbo, some old people around here, and all around the world haven't gotten over the fact that people of all colors are children of God, have rights, and we should respect each other." The old woman was trying to explain racism and how to treat people with proper respect. Jimbo was confused, but stopped his questions for the rest of the walk home. Jimbo went to his room, Emily went to her husband's workshop.

Emily adjusted her glasses, moved aside a saw, and opened the drawer in her husband's cluttered workbench. There she found an old journal written in her husband's poor handwriting. The first page was brief:

Figured it was time to start collecting thoughts for some future use. Perhaps this will be a method to communicate with my children, grandson, or future grandchildren as they grow older or at least be a commentary on current events and progress on the farm. It would be nice to have some profound thoughts on the condition of Man but I believe that this collection will be more representative of your run-of-the-mill common person. (Sorry, no greatness here.)

Emily read on for a few more pages then called for Jimbo. "Look what I found for you," she said as he stumbled through the narrow door.

"Grandma, what is it?"

"This is a gift to you from your Grandfather, she replied and handed over the dusty journal. Now you take care of that. It is a special gift for you," she cautioned.

"Yes ma'am," he replied in typical Southern courtesy.

Jimbo took his new prize to his tree house, the dogs gathered under him as he turned the pages. The encounter with the black man down at Lilly's market was fresh in his mind as he read:

I think that eventually the world moves towards justice. Often the pace is slow and measured in gen-

erations. However there are times when an individual is harmed and the forces to make amends push the process along and justice can be swift. An injustice cannot last forever because sooner or later someone will stand up and ask-- "what is the right thing to do." He will then follow that path and then others will follow him.

Do Right.
On the next page he saw:

How you handle disappointments and setbacks is an indication of where you take your life. It is easy to be knocked off your horse and stay down. It takes courage to get up one more time. In fact personal greatness can be achieved by doing nothing more than just getting back up time and again. There doesn't seem to be much glory here but it may well be a definition of a successful life--just keep getting up.

The young boy felt the presence of his grandfather, smiled, and turned the page:

Very simple philosophy: Do your best. If you can't approach a job or a relationship without offering your best, then you are saddled forever with a standard of mediocrity. Raising your standard of performance is not an easy task and there-

fore so few attempt it. However, you can excel--even with less talent--if you just pursue your best.

The young boy could remember the sound of the old man's voice now talking to him beyond the grave.

> *I think that God created us so he could love us. You don't have to earn His love, it is freely given, you only have to have faith and accept it. He loves you just as you are. You were born a spiritual being, a child of God, with God inside of you. Try to find God in all people. This will change how you view everyone.*

No one noticed, but Emily was slowing down. Her famous energy was gone. Lately she just felt tired.

After a while, Katherine said, "Mom you should go in to the doctor for a checkup just to be sure everything is alright."

"No, that is just a big waste of time and money. You sit and wait, then they don't tell you anything. I would rather stay out here on the farm than go to all the trouble of going to town."

"I think it is best to check you out. I'll go in with you. We will bring some magazines," Katherine said as she went to the phone to make an appointment.

The next week they were on their way to a big,

impersonal medical clinic. "Mrs. Patterson." called out a nurse's assistant.

"There goes privacy," Emily thought as she rose from the hard waiting room chair. Mrs. Patterson was poked, and stuck with needles.

"The test results should be back next week, so schedule a return visit. I'll go over those results with you," said a doctor who looked only a few years older than Jimbo. I think you are anemic, but we want to be sure what is causing it," the youthful physician said as he rushed out of the exam room.

"Take me home," is what Katherine heard as she rose to greet her mother-in-law. Bouncing up the driveway, the ladies could see Jimmy in the tractor shed and Jimbo up in his tree house, reading.

God gave us a gift of Free Will to make our own decisions. I encourage you to spend quiet time to listen and try to figure out God's will and plan for your life then make your decisions along those lines. Pray to find God's will for your life and the courage to follow it. If your free will lines up with His will, then you will find joy and a full life.

Grandchildren: as you grow think, be alert. How are you being formed? Is it from external forces? Are you formed by your peers, by TV, society's expectations? Or are you being formed internally? The internal presence of God is speaking to you, trying to guide you. Please listen internally *and not externally.*

The next several days the Pattersons put their famous worry trait in to high gear

Hank's tail had wagged the decision to build Emily's house first. Memories of the old house became blueprints for the new one, workers came for weeks, and the house grew up out of the ground like a crop. The house took Emily's mind off doctors and tests. Finally the day came for a return visit to town.

Katherine went with Emily into the exam room to wait some more for the youthful doctor.

"Mrs. Patterson, I hate to tell you this, but the tests indicate your anemia is due to cancer," is what the ladies heard. **Cancer**.

"We don't know yet where it is coming from or if it has spread until we do some more tests, and I'll schedule some scans for you at the hospital," he continued. The women remained silent, caught in their own thoughts and fears. Emily felt the weight of fatigue. Katherine felt sadness weigh on her. She was growing into a leadership role in the family. The ladies sought safety, and went home. Jimbo waved from his tree house as they bumped down the drive. He turned the page.

Happiness. We all seem to seek it and go to great lengths to claim it. I contend that most of us can't even recognize it when we see it. Mankind seems to be chasing its tail. We want it, don't recognize it, and don't appreciate it, and then want more. Our definition of happiness must be unrealistic and un-achievable and therefore we always come up short and disappointed. A goal is to fully appreciate the happiness that you have. This understanding will surely be a positive trail to more of what we seek.

The scans, tests and more doctor visits revealed more bad news. The Baptist ladies mobilized again. Food appeared from everywhere. The Patterson family was lifted on the shoulders of the church and com-forted by prayers. Emily rallied for a short time, her hair fell out. More prayers and she began to feel the beginning of her old strength and endurance.

Katherine followed a Patterson tradition when trouble hit the family. She didn't know it at the time, but a long string of women had done the same thing. First, a walk in the woods.

Katherine loved the little footpath that followed the creek. There was moss along one side and rounded river rocks in the creek bed shaped by years of water flowing over them. Sunlight filtered through the leaves in little rays making the path look magical. The air was pure, and no outside sound penetrated this sacred space. About 100 yards into the darkening woods she saw two ears very erect. A doe was watching, listening and smelling her approach. Katherine stopped and watched the deer. Both seemed frozen to their spots for a moment. The deer's tail flipped up, she wheeled and scampered deeper into the woods then, without effort, hopped a fence. Katherine also turned and later found herself on her knees with her hands in the rich, black dirt of her garden.

Mother Earth.

Planting, pruning, weeding were soothing activities, and calmed her fears for Emily and the family.

She had watched Emily's house get built and then felt the excitement as she and Jimmy reviewed plans for their new house. It seemed to take forever for the builder to finish their home. She heard every excuse a creative contractor could fabricate. Finally, after many walks and a lot of garden time, her house was finished. They had moved in, and Katherine was becoming more comfortable growing into the farm role that Emily had carried for so long.

Jimbo was off balance with his Grandmother ailing; he spent more time with his Grandfather's journal seeking comfort and answers

Take one day at a time. I've heard this advice

from so many sources. It's true. Most of the problems that I worry about never happen. Too much time and happiness is wasted worrying about the insignificant. Life goes on. You can't live more than a day at a time so why not enjoy it. If a day at a time is too tough, then try 5 minutes. Try to live in the present. Tomorrow will take care of itself. Read **Matthew 6:25-34** *"Therefore do not be anxious about tomorrow, for tomorrow will be anxious for itself. Let the day's own trouble be sufficient for the day." God is in the Present. Listen for Him.*

The Pattersons were preparing, but not talking about it. Preparing for life after she was gone. Emily's rally was brief, fatigue returned. Chemo rounds continued. Hope was stretched. Prayers multiplied. The family circled. Jimmy and Katherine made an extra effort to be gentle and nice to one another. Jimbo did his chores, and homework early so he could spend more time with his Grandmother. Emily worried about her family if she wasn't there to tend to them. She prayed for the land to be good to her son.

Prayer.

Grandchildren, I have a favorite fishing spot. Ask your Dad to show you where it is. It is one of the prettiest and quietest places on our farm. I encourage you to go there often, but don't take your fishing pole. Don't fish. Just sit. Quietly. Be in the presence of God and listen to what He wants to tell you at that moment, and then have the courage to live it.

As you learn to listen, you begin to feel the nudges and the voice of God directing and guiding you. It takes practice, but mainly clearing your mind of the distractions of the day; open your heart to Him.

One night after dinner and the "good nights," Emily drifted off to sleep, felt the outstretched hand of her husband, and could not return. Her death was not unexpected, but you can never fully prepare for it. The family, church and most of Cedar Grove were shocked by the news. The Patterson family rock was gone. Jimbo cried for days, then realized her words of wisdom, her lessons and his grand father's journal would guide him. He could feel them carrying him into an uncertain future. As he bounded out of his family's new house to go to the rich fields of the Patterson land, he looked up, and offered a *prayer* of thanks.

The young boy did what his father, grandfather and many before him had done. He went to the land. He walked through the fields feeling the rich dirt underfoot, then up the hills through the trees smelling the soil. Jimbo felt *Mother Earth* cradling him, comforting him. As he walked, he felt God in the soil and all around him. He remembered his father telling him that God was in everything and all around us. Jimbo found peace and courage on his walk through the Patterson land. He was ready to become a farmer.

Potts

They were brothers. The brass buttons on their denim overalls were shiny from wear, but that is where the similarities ended. Ocie was five years older at 23, Lem was 18. Ocie was large, hair receding, almost bald, not very bright. Lem had a full head of dirty shaggy brown hair, small frame, smart. Ocie was carrying the fishing rods and the worms. Lem tossed rocks randomly as they walked down the dirt path that served as a road during the late 1800's in what was to become prime farm country. Ocie tripped once in a while in the ruts made by wagon wheels, causing the rods to bounce.

"Watch where you are going Ocie, and don't drop them worms," warned Lem.

"Shut up and keep walking. We have a long way to go to that pond and it is going to get hot soon," he replied.

The South was beginning to heat up with humidity and a rising sun. Heat radiated off the dirt road. The boys moved on heading a few miles south of their home on Potts road named after their grandfather who had settled there, and claimed their land, built their house, cleared some of the land, and started farming.

Ocie and Lem were two of the five children of this generation. The others were girls. The Potts boys had the ambition to fish, hunt and farm. The Potts girls had already decided to move to town when they could.

"It sure is hot now Lem and feels like it could rain today."

"Not a cloud in the sky, Ocie, and we need to hurry along so we can catch a mess of fish and bring them back for supper."

"Let's make a shortcut to that pond," Ocie offered.

"There ain't no shortcut, just woods and poison ivy," Lem kept up his complaining.

The boys took an angle off the dirt path into the woods, Ocie leading with Lem complaining and reluctantly following. The woods were thick. It was easy to get lost, which they did after about an hour.

"Ocie you don't know where in blazes we are. I've been by this old oak tree three times now. You got us walking in circles."

"Shut up Lem, follow me. I know where I am, and where to get to that pond. You got anything to eat on you?"

The boys continued walking in the woods that once witnessed Chickasaws who actually knew where they were going. Eventually towards late afternoon the boys accidentally came out of the woods on a little rise that looked over a meadow that in future years would hold corn and soybean crops. At the edge of the meadow was a darkening of the soil that promised the start of the pond they were seeking.

"I told you I could find the pond," Ocie was getting more confident with each step.

"If we had stuck to the road, we would already have been there, fished, and been on our way home. You big goof," Lem replied. The banter continued for sometime.

Lem removed his hat, shook his hair and sat down on the grass to rest and look at the pretty meadow before him. Ocie was hatless, had no hair to shake, and lumbered to the ground next to his younger brother.

"Ocie, this sure is a pretty piece of land. A man needs some land to call his own."

"We got the Potts land, Lem. Since Pa passed on, you and me will split it up and you will have your own land."

"The girls don't plan to stay on the land so it will pass to you and me. I guess Ma has to sign some papers to officially pass it over to us though."

"Ma doesn't seem to want to do much of anything

these days since his passing, we shouldn't be bothering her just yet."

"Yes, we need to take all burdens off her as long as we can."

"I always wanted to be a farmer, and you know I'm as strong as a mule," Ocie was thinking ahead.

"I can handle a lot of the money figuring since I do that pretty good. As a team, we should do well on the Potts farm," Lem suggested.

"Hmmm, the Potts Farm, it just sounds good too," Ocie was ready to plow.

The boys were lost in the future when a raindrop plopped on Ocie's bare head. It startled him. Then it was like a bucket was being poured over the boys, the rain came so fast. They ran to the shelter of the trees.

"Ocie, we shouldn't be under trees in this lightening," Lem said. "If it hits one of these trees, we are goners."

"Yeah, you are right, let's run over to that rocky bluff over there above that creek. No trees there and that rock outcropping might keep us dry."

The rain was coming down in earnest now, but the creek was still almost dry. They hopped over it to reach the rocky bluff. Ocie chose the biggest rock to seek shelter. Lem moved to some rocks that jutted out to the left of where Ocie sat hunched under his boulder. The rain was coming down furiously with thunder and lightening all around. The boys were glad to be away from the trees, and watched as the little creek began to fill up and a current begin to flow. They watched as little rivulets from everywhere added its volume to the creek. The rain continued its furious pace and the creek became a re- spectable conduit of water. A growing rivulet came from behind Ocie's rock to join the creek, making the creek muddier in the process, Mud and water was added from the small hillside that sheltered the Potts boys. The boys tried to talk, but the rain drowned out their words.

Lem took his dirty, wet hat off, shook his hair, and put it back on. He turned his head to try to tell his brother something through the rain. At that moment the huge boulder sheltering Ocie fell from the hillside crushing him instantly. Lem knew he was dead, but he slipped through the mud anyway to offer any help he could. Ocie died there.

Lem had some problems. He couldn't budge either the boulder or his brother, so he walked. Lem walked in a direction he thought a farmhouse might be if he owned this land. After about an hour he saw smoke. The rain thankfully had stopped some time ago so the smoke was clearly visible and he walked towards it. The house was typical of the day: simple, small, and made from the wood of the surrounding trees. A dog barked a warning as he approached and a man with a shotgun opened the door.

"What do you want?" was his greeting.

"Mister, I need help bad. My brother is killed by a big rock over by your pond and creek."

"Well, son, you take me to him and we will figure out how a rock could kill your brother. Are you sure he's dead? What's your name, boy?"

Lem Potts, sir. A big rock fell on him."

"Hmmm Potts, huh? You any kin to them on Potts Road up north of here."

"Yes, sir. That's my family."

"Well, quite a walk from there."

The landowner and Lem retraced the boy's walk back to the creek to find his brother. The landowner's dog sniffed around the rock and Ocie. The dog was uncertain and went back to his master for comfort.

"There he is Mister."

"I don't think there is anything we can do to move this boulder today by ourselves. Tomorrow I'll hitch up my mule and get this rock off of him."

"I ain't leaving him here over night for the coyotes, coons and possums to get at him," Lem declared.

"I understand son. Here take my shotgun and I'll leave ole Duke here to keep you company. Now I'm going back to the house to get you some blankets and something to eat." The food and blankets added warmth to him for the long night. Duke was good company, and his dog smell probably kept the varmints away.

Early the next morning the landowner was there with his mule and a logging chain.

"Here slip that chain around the wide part of the rock," he said as Lem clambered up the muddy slope.

"Got it," he hollered down.

"Git up," the man instructed his mule and the rock rolled off the Potts brother. "Whoa." Another command." Son, I know this is hard for you, but we need to bury your brother. You can't stand guard every night."

"I can't get him home, so what can we do?" Lem asked.

"We can bury him here on my farm."

Together they hoisted Ocie up on the back of the mule, and balanced him the best they could.

"You sure you're brothers? This boy makes about three of you. Huffed the landowner."

"Yes, sir. He's my brother, but he was always bigger and he's five years older too."

They slowly took a tour of the farm.

"I like this little clearing by this road if it meets your approval for a cemetery," suggested Lem.

It was a pretty place on the top of a rise close to a dirt path that would become a road named after one of the pioneer families of the area. Some young oak trees provided shade and a few small cedars in a cluster gave the area character.

"I think this is a perfect place to lay your brother to rest."

Lem considered going home and seeking his mother's opinion, but remembered Ocie's suggestion to keep troubles off her shoulders.

Ocie Potts became the first resident to what would become the Potts Cemetery on a private farm. This cemetery would expand to include family members of neighbors and the Pattersons. Eventually it also became the ground of dispute between a future land owner named Bud, and a grandmother and her grandsons mowing across a line to keep the cemetery grounds looking nice.

"Mister, I need to go home now. Thank you for everything you have done for me and Ocie." Lem was thinking about the long walk home.

"Son, you come back any time to visit your brother, and come see me too."

Lem gathered the fishing rods over his shoulder, squared his hat, patted Duke's head, and went to say good-bye to his brother before heading home.

It seemed like a longer walk home, by himself, with no one to talk with. He realized that the Potts land would now be all his, but he was willing to split it many ways just to have Ocie back telling him to "Shut up."

The Potts dogs barked a warning and greeting at

the same time as he approached. They all ran towards him. He was thinking of what to tell the family. He saw his mother working in the garden, and went there. She was on her knees weeding around the peas and tomatoes. She rose, fluffed her long work dress and looked quizzically at her one son expecting two.

"Ma, I have something to tell you."

Randall

Down the road from the Pattersons, not far from Lilly's store, John Sloan owned a small farm. He mentored a young man for a few years, and his story became another part of the stories of Cedar Grove.

Randall's mother read the disturbing note he purposely left on his dresser face up. "I like to harm small animals and want to eat little kids." The note was decorated with ghoulish pictures of blood dripping off a knife and guns smoking. Randall's mother was concerned. She was going to tell her husband and her son's shrink.

About this same time John Sloan was having a stroke in Berlin, Germany. "Some vacation," he told his wife on his way to ICU.

Weeks later John and Randal were to meet at the Sloan farm in Western Tennessee, in Cedar Grove. John's left side was weak, and he needed some help.

Randall needed fresh air, a fresh perspective, and a new attitude.

"140+ acres is a lot of land to look after even when I was strong. Now, it will be much harder to fix fences and do the chores one-handed," he said. John and Randall were put together by a mutual friend who knew each could end up helping the other just by spending time together.

"You look a bit scrawny." Is what John first said jokingly and patting the boy's biceps. Randall took it in stride.

"Yes, but, I'm stronger than I look and can talk a chore done," he replied. The parents were hopeful but skeptical of this first meeting in their kitchen. They didn't know John Sloan very well and wondered what kinds of farm chores were awaiting their son.

"Trash?"

"Yes, trash along the road. If we don't pick it up, no one will," John explained to the boy.

Randall was hoping for something a little more exciting for his first day, but John had pride in his land and didn't like litter accumulating. Hopping in Sloan's John Deere 6 wheeled gator, they drove down the country road with Randall jumping off every few yards to pick up a beer can or fast food cup thoughtlessly tossed out a car window.

"Keep a close eye out for snakes," John warned.

Randall, at 15, was a good kid who happened to have attention deficit/hyper activity disorder (AD/HD). Medication helped, but he still was a handful for his parents and the school system. His psychiatrist knew he was smart and worked on behavior modification exercises. He was almost six feet tall, skinny, short cropped brown hair, and sometimes made an effort to grow out sideburns. Randall was a bundle of uncontrolled energy often looking to shock those around him with his thoughts, writings or words. John had the patience of someone who had already raised three children. He didn't shock easily.

The back of the gator filled with trash so they headed back to the house. "Let's take a tour," John suggested. Followed by four dogs, they drove across the pastures exploring the land. Randall was at the wheel driving carefully, working hard to be mature and focus on the task at hand.

"This is fun. Never had the chance to be free to drive across open land," Randall shouted above the engine noise.

"When we are finished with the tour, if we have time, I'll introduce you to the horses," John shouted back.

"Horses? You have horses?" Now the kid showed interest.

Running out of land and daylight they turned toward home.

"Next time, no trash and we will concentrate on the horses," John said.

"Great, Always wanted to be a cowboy." Was the response.

On the ride home in John's red pick up farm truck, Randall kept up a continuous chatter. Mainly he was performing comedy routines. He liked watching the comedy channel then adding his own twist to the routines and performing them for John.

"Stop, I'm going to wet my pants if you keep it up, " John laughed too hard. "At least let me catch my breath. "If you give me another stroke because of these jokes, it won't be funny," John said.

"OK but I wanted to try these out before I use the jokes in shop class tomorrow," Randall explained, laughing along with John.

When John dropped the boy off at his house he couldn't help but notice how the parents gave their son a close look for any recent damage.

The next weekend found John and his beat up farm truck in the driveway of Randall's house waiting for him to down the last of his lunch. He emerged with a black Johnny Cash shirt and a black cap with a skull on it.

"Hi Randall, How was your week? John asked.

"Good. Do you like Johnny Cash? I think he is so cool," the boy went on.

"Were you named Sue?" John asked.

"No, I shot a man in Reno once just to watch him die," was the reply.

John and Randall proceeded to quote Johnny Cash song lyrics with Randall running circles around the older man.

"OK, OK you spend too much time listening to music," John gave up.

On the drive to the farm they listened to a Johnny Cash CD while Randall went through another comedy routine. "You're killing me, stop," John pleaded.

They parked the red truck and hopped into the John Deere green and yellow gator. Chased by the dogs, they drove up to the barn. The barn was fairly new, built by a local Mennonite clan with a tin roof. It had three stalls and a locked tack room where the saddles and grain were kept.

"One thing about horses, John began, is that before we play with them, you first have to shovel."

"Shovel?"

"Here, this one should fit you." "Just start with that first stall and shovel the manure into the spreader that is around the corner there," John instructed.

"Oh, this is fun. I bet Roy Rogers never did this," Randall began complaining.

"When you finish with the first stall, there are two more with your name on them," John was unfazed, and wanted clean stalls.

After the manure management lesson, they went to the round pen where John introduced the boy to the three horses. "Shiloh here is a gelding, and if you don't do your chores around here, you'll be one too," now John was joking, but Randall wasn't sure yet what a gelding was so missed the humor. "Lacy is a mare and she tends to be the alpha horse of this little herd and the momma of this filly." Behind John a smaller horse with a white star blaze on her forehead peeked over his shoulder. The filly was hesitant, but curious about Randall. She sniffed in his direction, ears erect. "Wow, you are a beauty," Randall said. "What's her name?"

"She doesn't have one yet," John replied. "Maybe you can come up with one."

The curiosity was getting the best of the filly and she walked from behind John to stand in front of Randall so she could get a good look and sniff. Randall saw a white sock on her rear right foot, long brown mane and tail. Her body was a dark brown, not black, but very dark brown, her feet were excellent. She snorted at Randall and the moisture from her nose sprayed the boy. "She just blew snot on me," he protested.

"No she didn't, you sissy," She is checking you out and had to sneeze. Lucky she didn't kick you," John said.

"She is a beauty and we will get along in time," the boy said. He rubbed her on the white of her head.

Randall spent the week thinking about the filly and names for a horse. Most of the names seemed to mimic heavy metal bands. He still spent too much time up in his bedroom playing video games, isolated from his family.

"Those video games either make you violent or desensitize you to violence," John said on the way to the farm on the following week.

"Nah, they are harmless," Randall defended.

"Look at Columbine and all those other shootings, kids in black. I bet you can trace some of that violence back to stupid video computer games," John countered.

"I think more was going on in those kids than just games," Randall responded.

"Still, I think getting outside is better than being isolated with violence.

"Now, I agree with you on that." Randall closed the conversation then moved in to one of his comedy routines.

"After you shovel shit, then what do you want to do?" John asked.

"Play with Murphy," Randall quickly replied.

"Murphy? Who's that?" John inquired.

"The filly. She is always getting into something like Murphy's Law, so I thought the name fit," Randall was grinning.

"OK Murphy it is," John agreed.

The filly threw her head up, eyes wide, scared. "No you can't move that fast and jerky. See you scared her," John advised.

"Sorry girl,"

Randall calmed her down and started over.

"Your movements around a horse have to be slow and deliberate. Fast movements are going to get her scared. You need to slow down," John was trying to teach.

"This hyperactivity disorder gets me every time," Randall complained.

""If you are going to get Murphy to trust you, then you are the one who will have to change, she is hard-wired as a flight animal. So slow it down. Calm down." John advised.

Randall took a deep breath, picked up the brush, and started again. Muphy twitched her ears, calmed her eyes and also relaxed. The boy and the horse were making progress. She leaned into the brush. He whispered to her.

"Success builds on success," John was saying on the trip home with Randall.

"Next week we pick up where we left off in the round pen with Murphy. You catch her, then brush her out. She likes that and soon won't mind the catching or the halter. Remember to move slowly as you put the halter over her head and be gentle with her ears."

"This is fun. No one I know plays with a horse on week ends." he replied.

"Better than video games?" John asked

"Absolutely."

Next week John watched as Randall hopped over the gate leading into the horse pasture. All three horses looked up for a moment from their grazing to see what was going on. Murphy's head popped up, ears erect at full attention. She nickered when she recognized Randall.

"Now that is special," John declared.

"That's my girl," the boy said.

Murphy came on at a trot with her mane flowing up and down with each step, tail held high. She came to a stop in front of Randall breathing loudly. The boy put his arms around her neck and held her until her breathing calmed and her ears relaxed.

"I think that horse likes you," John said.

"I've been thinking about her all week," replied Randall.

"All week? What about school and those famous video games up in your room?"

"School was fine. I told my friends about Murphy. They don't understand. The computer games aren't as fun as this, so I hang out more with the family now and tell them about the farm."

"That's good. Get out of your room. Enjoy

your family. Be a good big brother to that sister of yours."

"Yes, and I can stir up the dogs too."

"Stay out of trouble, son. See you next week."

"Jenny we have a new partner on the farm," John was explaining to his friend who came out most weekends to the farm with her family. He went on to tell her about Randall and how he was learning about horses.

"You can really help him there, and teach him things about how to handle a horse," John said. Jenny had grown up with horses, was an accomplished rider and very experienced in all things to do with horses. She and her kids all got to like Randall after the first introduction.

"Hey, do you babysit?" was her question.

"Ahh—Umm, yeah, I guess if it isn't during school hours." Randall replied.

"Good, I always need a babysitter," Jenny said.

"Randall, come on man. Take a hit. This pot is good." His friend was holding out a rolled marijuana cigarette to him.

"No thanks. I don't want that stuff any more," Randall replied.

"Getting Chicken on me, man?" was the reply.

"No, not chicken, another species, getting horse on you," Randall said, which confused his friend. "Listen, if I get caught, my folks will kill me, we both get kicked out of school and I will be grounded from going out to the farm and seeing my horse. That's too much to risk." Explained Randall as he got up and walked away.

"Murphy is looking good these days. You have earned her trust. Look at how she lowers her head and has that one ear turned toward you," John was commenting as Randall worked the young filly in the round pen.

"Yes, I think she is finally getting the idea here," Randall said with a big grin.

"Hey, that horse looks like a veteran, who has been doing all the advanced training?" Jenny came around the corner of the barn, and was impressed by what she saw.

"Jenny, can you work with the kid here for a little while, I've run out of expertise," John said. The boy and the woman worked together for the rest of the afternoon, and the filly continued to improve.

"She's about ready to ride," said Jenny.

"Wow, that will be so cool," the boy replied.

John consulted with Jenny and they decided to let all the horses out into the big cow pasture because the grass in the smaller horse pasture was just too sparse. The horses took tentative steps past the gate like they might be in forbidden territory. Then they got comfortable with the freedom and ran up the hill. "That's beautiful," Randall exclaimed.

"Yep, now they can live like real, natural horses for a while," Jenny replied.

Randall didn't come out to the farm the next weekend because his parents found that he skipped classes for a few days. Grounding him from the farm was the most effective punishment they could come up with. Life on the farm continued and the horses wandered between the smaller horse pasture to the big pasture

Murphy, the filly, was exploring away from the herd. She moved down the hillside into the swampy area. John Sloan counted horses the next morning and came up with one short. For the next several days he toured the farm looking for the filly. Jenny came out that weekend and so did Randall so there were many eyes looking for the horse. "Let's walk the swampy area," Jenny suggested. She, Randall and a few of the dogs spread out over the large area. John drove the gator. For the first hour nothing was spotted. "I wonder if she found a way off the property," offered Randall. "No, I doubt that," John replied. "Let's keep looking." John was slightly ahead of Jenny and Randall in the gator and saw a brown hump off to his right. He called one of the dogs that went straight to the "hump." John drove closer and soon could clearly see that he had found Murphy. He hollered to the others. Randall ran to him then fell to his knees, crying. Jenny arrived and gathered Randall in her arms, holding and comforting the grieving boy. They examined the dead horse. "Looks like he got stuck here then broke his hip." Said Jenny. "Yes, and his leg is also broken right there too," John said. Randall had a hard time looking. "Since she is partially submerged that is probably why the buzzards didn't gather," John surmised. "Well, it doesn't look like it stopped the coyotes," Jenny said. Randal was moving a sob to a wail. "Jen, why don't you start taking Randall back to the barn," John suggested as all three got to their feet. It was a quiet walk to the barn as each was into his own thoughts. "Goodbye Randall, I'm so sorry," Jenny said.

"Sorry Randall, think of those good times," John added as Randall drove off to go home.

"OK back to work," John said. He cranked up his John Deere tractor and Jenny began to walk back to the swamp. Once there they tied a tow rope around the horse and pulled her to dry ground. Then readjusted the rope and lifted the beast with the front end loader and hauled her to a suitable burying spot.

"I think this will work. Why don't you take a breather and I'll start digging a hole with the tractor," John said.

"Sure, but dig a little more over here and away from that creek," suggested Jenny. For the next several hours the green and yellow tractor scraped and dug a hole big enough for a horse. Using the front end loader again, John lifted the filly and tried to gently lower her into the grave. The hole should have been bigger. Then for the next couple of hours dirt was placed over the grave, and Murphy became one with the land.

"I'm sad," Jenny said.

"I am too. It has been a long day," said John.

Randall's grades had steadily improved, his college test scores were excellent. He was keeping out of trouble, communicating with his family and his teachers. Murphy was still guiding his behavior

John Sloan

John was a city man who bought a farm and leased the land to Jimmy Patterson with a handshake agreement. Right after buying the land he and his wife took a trip to Germany. Then he had a stroke. His story.

My brain exploded, and I spent the next week flat on my butt in the ICU in a German hospital. I missed Bubba and the Boys down at Lilly's Market in downtown Cedar Grove, TN, 38321. I am writing this so I can tell my story once, and for you, Bubba since you usually fall asleep and out of your chair. The intent is to share my story with Bubba and the Boys sitting around Lilly's. If Rednecks or Germans get insulted or offended, then they just didn't get the joke. I can now sort of move my left arm, but my fingers don't work very well, so I am typing with one right hand finger---that is slowwww. I have noticed that people here speak foreign. It is close to a group of Yankee tourists stopping by Lilly's seeking directions to Paris Landing, 38307 or Parker's Crossroad, 38358.

Time and a lot of hand movements. At least speaking to a Yankee, both parties are working off the base of English. With the foreigners, we are just winging it. I wonder if they call me a "Yankee" behind my back? You can't understand them. I have noticed that the Germans like their "W's" they are like a ton of crazed Elmer Fudd's going around saying W's" like: where are you, you wascally wittle wabbit. I'm getting wery, wery mad at you. It is odd at first, but you do adapt. It is also like a time warp has put you in a German scrabble game where wevery player has wayy too many w's to play, so they toss out w's wevery chance they get if you aren't wareful, then you can get hurt by flying w's. they called me Mr. Weed instead of Reed. After a couple of days of being Mr. Weed, I began to feel like a big marijuana plant.........my wife, doesn't like the way I use w's. I call her the wicked, wevil wife. For some weason that offends her. She should re-read page 1 . Ooooppppss I said "re-read." that is wery,wery close to "re-rent." I was saying the word "re-rent" when my brain exploded. Bubba, I know you are now trying to say "re-rent a hundred times in a row to see if your brain will explode; and you can get a lot of attention========Don't do it!!! You are tempting Fate. Give it time. Your brain will explode in its own due time. Please be sure Harley is tied when you black out...................

While in the German hospital, I got bored. Twice I played cupid, but to no avail. The ER doctor was the most beautiful woman in the universe. I would gladly have another stroke just to receive another one of her examinations. I thought she, Dr. Sara, would be a perfect fit for the ICU doctor, Dr. Yuri. He also thought that she was beautiful, but I had to sell him to her. I told Dr. Sara that Dr. Yuri wasn't the most handsome guy in the world, but that he had no bad habits, and was trainable. I thought those were good qualities, but Dr. Sara was not terribly impressed. Later, as

I was pushing Dr. Yuri to make his move and ask her out, I found a flaw in the plan. She was married! Well cupid and stupid are twins. Bummer! The marriage detail discouraged Dr. Yuri, but not me. I persisted to get them together. To date I think it remains an idea only in my head, and as you know, that head exploded and isn't a good reliable way to view the world. I was told that when you have a stroke that your behavior changes. It is possible that I will get confused, have bad judgment and be very impulsive. Bubba, that describes you to a T. It also sounds a lot like an 18 year old. So this stroke may be a "do-over" to be 18 again! What a sweet deal…. Also, when I get caught doing something very stupid, I can play my ACE card, which is to say, "What do you expect? I'm dain bramaged." That is an automatic "get out of jail card." However don't overuse the card. My wicked wevil wife fails to find it humorous after the 100th time I used it. I also played cupid with the very pretty nurse, Katarina, and the world famous and brilliant Dr. Schmidt. But there was another minor problem. This time HE was married. It is hard to play cupid with all these marriages in the way. I should have better judgment, but the stroke gave me bad judgment, so I started playing cupid—which was stupid. I called him "World famous and Brilliant." because he told me his job was to get me better and to get me home. That was music to my ears and earned him the brilliant distinction. I still think the Katarina and Dr. Schmidt match is a good one.

They took away the "bad blue ball." It was supposed to be rolled up and down my left arm to stimulate the nerves, but that got old soon, so I devised another use for it: throwing it at nurses and doctors. I got pretty good at it with almost pinpoint accuracy. A problem was that after I threw it, I couldn't walk to go get it, so I had to sweet talk a nurse to go fetch the "bad blue ball" for me and I would promise-- actually lie—that I wouldn't hit her again, which I would. I missed once and knocked down the IV pole of the patient in the bed next to me. He moved to another room, which was fine with me since he snored like Bubba. That "bad blue ball" got me into a lot of trouble. When they took it away from me, I got bored again.

One morning I woke up to a nurse with a razor at my neck. I was getting a shave in bed, but the razor was making me nervous. I didn't make any fast moves and she didn't slit my throat. A good deal for both of us. Then she proceeded to "refreshen" me, which is like having a sponge bath in bed. She raised one arm and said let's refreshen this "wing", then she refreshened the other arm/wing. Later the sponge moved down my chest heading towards the private zone, and she said now we refreshen this "wing." I never knew I had one wing much less THREE wings! At the end of the process I was fully "refreshened." One morning I was awakened by a very happy and pretty nurse to do the refreshen routine, She cheerily asked me to roll over on my side, which I thought she was going to refreshen my back. Then she said "temperature" and I felt a thermometer invade my butt. Ouch! Not fair! She left the room before I could protest. This thermometer is one that beeps when it is finished. So there I lay, beeping out of my butt. Finally the beeping drew attention and an army of nurses showed up to stop the beeping and withdraw the offending noise maker. After that I began to negotiate under a wing to take the next temperature.

After a stroke it is recommended to begin physical therapy as soon as possible. The bad blue ball probably scared the therapists away for a few days. Then they got me. Even before the stroke my body didn't bend that way. I started calling them physical terrorists. Everybody but them thought that was a funny title. I miss my bad blue ball.

People ask me if I know what caused the stroke or if I had any symptoms. I have thought back on this and have a good idea as to what triggered the stroke. It was too much culture. Out here in Cedar Grove we don't get much culture. My wife dragged me to two art museums, an old castle and a couple of old churches. My culture meter went off the charts and my brain exploded. So Bubba, beware of too much culture. I doubt that you are at risk based upon your history. Going to Hooters does not count as culture. Nor does the Buck and Bass shop. Stuffed animals are not art. Your Elvis painting on black velvet doesn't count either.

I appreciated the effort the German doctors and nurses made to speak English. All in all they did a fine job in spite of their desire to sprinkle "ws" everywhere. One day a doctor was stitching in an inline thing to continuously monitor my blood pressure. In the process he stuck himself with the needle, which I thought was a bit of an irony. But, the stick did concern him in this day of AIDS. He said, Mr. Weed, I stuck myself, do you mind if we do an HIWee test?" I had a difficult time understanding what HIWhee meant. Finally I realized their love for "ws" and that he was asking me to take an HIV test. I agreed to it to calm his fears. They took some blood and left for the lab. A few minutes the doctor returned with a concerned or confused look on his face. Negative is "bad" and "positive" is good. Usually, unless it applies to a blood test, then the meanings are reversed. It is "Positive" or good to have a "negative" result on an HIV test. He pondered the quandary for what seemed like an eternity leaving me to think that it was possible that I actually did have HIWhee. That was a sobering moment. I couldn't take his pause and stammering about so I asked, "Do I have HIWhee?" He said no. The test is negative, which is positive news for you. We both took a deep breath and relived the confusing moment with me asking for the umpteenth time about the test really being "negative," and how that meant "positive" news. Good and bad reversed in two languages made me worry about HIWhee for the first time. The discussion wore us both out. As he left the room, I nailed him with the "bad blue ball."

Then there was my battle with the pee bottle or

you could call it lessons in gravity. Bubba, all your life you have been told, "don't pee in the wind." Now I recommend, "don't pee uphill." The results are the same. After the stroke I couldn't walk very well, and they didn't want me to walk to the bathroom. So, I got this nice plastic jug with a big hole at the top and a lid to snap over it, simple, you might think, but you are naïve to the laws of gravity. I filled the first jug right off, then filled the second one. I put them both on a stand next to the bed. Then gravity attacked, and for some reason, both jugs fell to the floor.....Bubba, you would be surprised how fast and far a gallon of pee will spread on a level floor. About this time Helmut, the aid, arrived "Mr. Weed, we have a little problem here. Then as he got the mop and surveyed the job it became "a big problem. He worked with the words of "big" and "problem," and it became, "Mr. Weed we have a massive disaster." I thought that was overstating it a bit, but then he was the one doing the clean up. Then Helmut, Jr. showed up and they talked about the "Massive disaster" and who had to clean it up. After a while the floor was clean. Jr. left and came back with something that looked like a pole used in pole vaulting. He opened the door and said, "Mr. Weed-pause-then the dreaded word "catheter" he pronounced it proudly as "ca-THE-ter. Anyway you say it, it still hurts when they insert it. So after much pain I graduated from the pee bottle to a bag attached to my penis. I missed being at Lilly's in downtown Cedar Grove, 38321 about then.

For the next several days whenever anyone came into my room I cautioned them to be "wery, wery careful." I could imagine someone getting entangled between me and the bag. I knew that a ca-THEter being ripped out couldn't feel good regardless of the language. Finally a couple of nurses got tired of being "wery, wery careful, and they took it out, which feels slightly less painful than going in. Now I was back to the dreaded pee bottle, but "free at last!" It sounds simple to position the pee bottle down hill, then let loose, but you are lying horizontally, and can only use one hand. It ain't easy, Bubba. Some days I missed the big opening. Some days I got downhill wrong and was going uphill. The daily results were the same: pee everywhere! I thought I had made every possible mistake on using the pee bottle, but I forgot about the "firehose effect." One morning I got the bottle going down hill, got good aim at the opening, but could hold only one thing at a time with my one good hand. Since I thought I had the stars and the pee bottle aligned, I started going. Almost immediately I felt what was becoming all too familiar, a warm wet sensation spreading around me. I forgot about the "firehose effect." Using my good hand to hold the bottle there was no direct guidance on my penis, so when the pressure came, it aimed all over the place. Now I know why there are two men stationed on the end of a spurting firehose. I really needed my left hand. You could also attach the pee bottle by a hook handle on the bed. Well, that hook is tricky, and gravity carried that bottle to the floor several more times. Helmut was not happy, but the catheter did not arrive, there IS a God. Gravity got me again one morning. I filled the bottle without incidence, hooked it in the bed rail and relaxed. I thought it would be more comfortable if I raised the head part of the bed. So I pressed the simple up button and half the bed began to rise. As half goes up to support my head, the other half of the bed goes down to keep some semblance of balance. As fate would have it, as the rails went up and part of it went down, I realized the pee bottle was hooked to the rail going DOWN. Gravity again! Helmut was not happy. Life will be good if I never see another pee bottle. Gravity was winning. Then when I thought I had done everything possible with that bottle, one morning I heard the splash sound of pee on the floor. This morning I had forgotten to open the snap lid over the big opening hole. Pee was splashing everywhere—again! Finally, I quit using the pee bottle and just peed on the floor. It was easier for me. I eliminated the middleman, and the result was the same. Helmut was not overjoyed, but it was hard to keep Helmut happy anyway. Besides I was leaving the joint. I had discovered that there was not razor wire around the hospital perimeter and I also learned they did not have guard dogs, so I said "goodbye" and left for America, leaving behind the cursed pee bottle. Bubba, don't mess with gravity.

We escaped Berlin only to be stranded for 8 hours' plane delay in Amsterdam. Home seems like a very long way away. I miss Bubba and the boys at Lilly's market in downtown Cedar Grove, TN, 38321.

A lot of people are saying they are praying for me, and that is nice. While waiting in Amsterdam a good Samaritan helped me from the wheelchair to a seat in the busy airport. We started talking, and I told him about my stroke. He asked if he could pray for and with me. I didn't think it would hurt, so I said, "sure." Then he asked if he could touch me. I'm glad he asked otherwise I would have freaked out. So, he lays hands on my shoulder and offers a fervent prayer in the busy Amsterdam airport. When he finished, I slowly raised my weak left arm up in the air. He was surprised, but convinced he had just performed a miracle on a crippled man. I didn't tell him that my left arm always worked a little. I figured he was feeling pretty good, so it was best to let him keep smiling in wonderment. The crowd parted like the Red Sea, and I wheeled towards my gate and the waiting airplane to take me back home to the farm.

Somewhere over the Atlantic it was time for my medication, which has to be injected into my stomach. I was prepared to do it myself, but my wicked wevil wife talked to a flight attendant who made a very public announcement for a health professional to come forward. Soon a husband and wife, both nurses, from the states were hovering over me, arguing. Each wanted to do the honors and felt more qualified than the other, thus the argument. I looked up meekly from my seat and tried clicking my heels like Dorothy in the Wizard of Oz. It didn't work. Finally, an alpha nurse emerged, and I felt the plunge of a needle in my belly at 30,000 feet.

I find that a lot of people other than the Amsterdam miracle worker have been praying for me. At last count I had Baptists, Methodists, Catholics and a few Amish tossing up prayers. I'm pretty sure it helps. I am recovering very fast.

Upon arrival in the good ol USA, I promptly entered another hospital for rehab. It was time to learn to walk again. Listening to "y'all" and "fixin to" and other Southern sayings was music to my ears. There wasn't a flying W anywhere to be heard. Elmer Fudd was left in Germany. So was the "bad blue ball."

I had nothing to throw at the doctors and nurses here at home. I also found that the physical therapists on this side of the ocean didn't appreciate being called "physical terrorists" either. One particular guy even brought an auto battery with jumper cables to my room to emphasize his point that he had terrorist potential. We quickly came to an understanding. Eventually I relearned to walk, not dance, but I couldn't dance very well before the stroke either. I asked around, and found that this hospital also did not have razor wire or guard dogs, so I left.

Home on the farm was sweet, and I decided that I needed a project. A project would keep my damaged brain busy and keep me out of trouble—temporarily. The farm has dogs, cats, horses, cows, but no chickens. That's right, no chickens and that seemed like an easy critter to maintain plus you get fresh eggs in return for a little work. The first thing you do is build a house for them. Most people call this a coop. However, I constructed a chicken *castle*. On wheels. The construction phase was difficult for a guy whose left side barely functions. I could stand, walk slowly, but the motor skills of my left hand were very primitive. So the scene was me balancing on my good right leg, using my left leg, forehead and wobbly right elbow to hold a board in place while I used a power drill to screw it generally in place. I gave up on a hammer after whacking my left hand multiple times since it couldn't hold a nail steady. Thankfully a few friends and Randall pitched in on the tricky parts and the chicken castle began to take shape. I built it on top of a cheap trailer. In fact all the components were cheap. The idea was to be able to move the castle to other areas of a pasture to fresh bugs and grass for the future birds. It kinda worked that way until the trailer broke down. Finally the chicken *castle* was complete. A big door for humans. A little door for birds. A tin roof to keep every one dry. A broom handle served as a roost. It was a castle indeed. Although, in reality, it looked a lot like a hillbilly outhouse on wheels. The only thing lacking was the birds. Now you might think it easy to find chickens in the country, but try it once. First, you must locate a "chicken man." I found such a guy about 30 miles away. We agreed to meet at a middle point, which was in a parking lot of a bank in a small town. Tony, but I think everyone calls him Bubba, drove up in a noisy beat up Datsun. He had his dirty ball cap turned to the side, but didn't look like a rapper. He opened his trunk to reveal three squirming onion sacks, which I found to be crammed with full grown chickens. Rhode Island Reds. Cuckoo Morans. Black Alsolorps. They couldn't be comfortable traveling like that. We transferred the birds to the back of my truck like drug dealers doing a transaction. He went West, I went East. No cops. No shots fired. A good deal. I filled up the feeders and waterers. Then with a little fanfare, known only to the birds and myself, I opened the bags. The chickens walked out, fell out and got out of the bags. They got upright, then got right to cackling and attacking each other, which I learned is establishing the pecking order. I suspect learned behavior from Washington. The birds and I bonded. I closed them up at night, let them out in the early morning, gathered their eggs, kept them fed and watered. I also kept the dogs and chickens apart.

One fateful day. The chickens were out "free ranging," peacefully eating bugs and things, clucking happily, a HallMark moment. The dogs were contained in the garage. My wicked, weevil wife returned from shopping, clicked the garage door opener, and like a shot out of a canon came our old arthritic black lab. Like a black laser, he shot for my favorite chicken, It took only one bite. I hope death was quick. It was hard to tell because feathers were flying everywhere. I had read somewhere that an effective way to cure a chicken killing dog is to tie the dead bird around his collar and chain the dog up for a few hours for him to think about it. I tried it. Old Jake had his ears and tail tucked, and looked truly sorry after 2 hours. The punishment didn't work. Jake became a chicken killing machine.

He decimated my first flock. I reflocked, and he killed those with even more efficiency. The old, arthritic, hobbled dog, who could barely get up was a chicken killer nonpar. I restocked my flock several times with clandestine meetings with Tony, the chicken man,

Then there is the story about why the chickens quit laying eggs and how the chicken killing dog murdered another one in the middle of a birthday party full of 12 year old girls who are now scarred for life.

It is busy out on the farm. No wonder I started up a side business of makin' moonshine............

Today I am down to one bird, and Tony won't return my calls. Jake, his muzzle white and back legs crooked, is unrepentant.

A side effect of a stroke, which my doctor failed to tell me, is that it is possible to have a seizure. I guess I had one the day I was driving into town on hwy 70, a two-lane highway. I felt something coming on, so I slowly put on the brakes and pulled to the side. As I focused, I realized I was carefully parked facing oncoming traffic. Even a bit dain bramaged, you know that ain't good. So, I looked all eight ways and carefully pulled forward and into the proper lane deciding to turn into a church parking lot about a quarter of a mile down the road on the right hand side. I missed the turn in and kept on going. Shortly after that a big tree jumped right out in front of me! My truck hit it with vigor. I awoke with smoke drifting in the cab. I'm thinking I passed out, hit something, now I'm on fire, so this isn't a good day. After waiting a while for the truck to explode, a good Samaritan stopped to see if I was dead or bleeding. He seemed disappointed when neither was happening, but did tell me that the truck was not on fire. I learned that there is a powder inside the airbags, and when they go off, that powder looks like smoke. I was still a bit dazed when that tree jumped out at me, but I remember telling the HWY patrol officer very clearly that I had not been drinking that morning even though he didn't buy my jumping tree story. Later you couldn't see the tracks of the truck coming off the road, but the tree was between me and a nice house on the side of hwy 70. I guess that is a lesson not to buy a house on the side of a highway or plant a lot of trees around it if you do. I also learned that if you hit a tree with vigor in your truck and total both the tree and the truck, they give you a new one. Truck that is. The state, in an effort to protect its citizens won't let people who have had a stroke drive until after 6 months and until they pass a recertification, which I did. The state also denies driving privileges for 6 months to anyone who has had a seizure. I waited the time out, and now terrorize the roads again.

Billy Berkley

Billy was always a hard worker, and preferred to work alone so he could think. In his younger days he mainly worked construction until the scaffolding accident put him in the hospital. After that, he drifted back home to Cedar Grove, moved into his mother's old home, which was basically a shack, after she died. He started raising chickens and a garden. He never married, but went to church every Sunday and got the job mowing the yard and doing odd jobs there. Billy was trustworthy, recited Scripture to himself, the birds and anyone in listening range. He was a thinker too. When he drove the lawn mower or did his little mindless chores, he was thinking.

Billy: *You can't trust your mind. Your intellect will take you to worldly directions and goals. It will then do great rationalizations telling you this is the right path until you actually think it is. But don't be deceived. Your mind takes you to the false world. Listen to your heart. Open it to the Holy Spirit and to Grace. That will lead you to God. You must die to your intellect and live again in your heart, making room for the Holy Spirit. We use our minds to chase false gods of materialism and rationalize and convince ourselves that this is the right path, but truly we are running from eternal life in the process.*

God gave us free will. That is a powerful gift, and I think most of us misuse it. He also gave us His only Son who died for our sins that this free will did for us. Most folks go to hell from their own choosing. They choose to reject the infinite love of God and use the gift of free will to choose sin and a path away from Him. I see it happening all around me, but I can't help those people. They have eyes, but can't see, ears, but can't hear. I pray for them, but the gates of hell are open wide and people are streaming in. I think this grieves God. He loves them, and I imagine His hand outstretched to them as they reject Him time and again. The One who created us so He could love us eternally doesn't want to lose us to hell for eternity. It is sad.

He switched tools from mowing to trimming the many bushes around the church. It was harder to hold the trimmer and wave to the people driving by, so he preferred mowing. He was like a farmer in that he was careful to mow in straight lines. He also thought as he trimmed.

Billy: *I hear about people always talking about television shows and it seems to me that most folks watch hours and hours of sex, violence and stuff. I don't have a TV so I don't really know. But I think this time could be better spent with the Bible, or just being outside in Nature in God's land.You can't know God better without putting in the time and effort. I bet some folks, when they die, wish they had spent more time with the Lord than with the TV set.*

"Hey Billy, the place is looking good. Feel free to mow on down into my yard, my grass needs cutting too." Fred, the next door neighbor often made this request.

"Now Fred, You know the Pastor here only gives me enough time to mow and tend to the church yard. I'll be sure to mow right to your property line though," replied Billy.

Fred went back to his house. Billy went back to his thinking.

Billy: *Prayer is important. It is like talking to my best friend. I hope other people take the time to develop a daily prayer life and talk to God throughout the day. It is another way to diminish yourself and expand Him in your life. God is Love.What better thing to do during the day than have a talk with Love? The more we pray, the more we will feel Grace and the Holy Spirit working and dwelling in us.*

Billy adjusted his helmet, wiped off some sweat,

and prepared to gather the tools of the day. He looked at his handiwork with pride and knew the church members would be proud of their little church in the country. He was ready for a break and conversation down at Lilly's.

Johnsons

The Johnsons, all six of them, came from North Carolina. Many families had done the same, stopping along prime land in what was to become Tennessee. The Johnsons were either more picky or stubborn so they kept moving west into Chickasaw Territory. Crossing the big Tennessee River almost stunted their trip, but a few miracles held them together and they made it to the other side.

Ben Johnson was a big, powerful man, and the family heeded his leadership as strangers helped them along. Martha, his wife, seemed to be pregnant most of her adult life. She had babies, but most if them died in or shortly after childbirth, which was common of the time. This weakened her and made her sickly. The trip just about killed her, but Ben said to move on, so they did. It was 1790 and they found a pretty hillside isolated in West Tennessee which later would become part of Cedar Grove. They were one of the Pioneer families of this area, and in 1821 a real county would be formed with their land at the edge of it. Since the Johnsons were there first, they named a road after themselves and Ben pretty much did what he wanted. The Indians noticed the increase of the North Carolinians and most of them scattered before Andrew Jackson could round them up for the Trail of Tears march. The Johnsons controlled their edge of the county. Martha was the first to give up. She died, and was buried near their log house. This was before the Potts cemetery had been created, but now the Potts cemetery is well populated with the descendants of the original Johnsons. Ben was left with four children, two boys and two girls and no immediate family and no known neighbors. He was in a fix. Arthur, Ben, Jr., Carol and Deborah were his to raise. He and Martha started naming their children by the alphabet, but she gave up well before they got to Zebulon or Zelda.

"Girls get your things together, we are going to look for a settlement," was his order for them. Ben had decided that his family needed neighbors. The isolation was fine for him, but not good for the children.

"Boys, I'll be back, check our traps, was the order for them.

He slung a gun and his pack over his shoulder and started walking. There was not a road or real trail so

Ben followed what he called a game trail where deer and other animals had made their way through the underbrush and into the forest. The girls rushed to put clothes and favorite things in their packs and trotted after him. Ben always found or killed his food on the trail, so there was no need to carry extra weight. Two days later they rounded a hill that would become a site for a civil war skirmish called Parker's Crossroads. Nathan Bedford Forrest was a key figure in this battle, and he reportedly got surrounded by the Yankees and gave the famous order to "Charge in both Directions!" A few tents were huddled together around a campfire. Ben walked towards it. There was a mixture of men, women and children of all ages mingling around the tents and fire. Ben's girls were shy and tentative, but Ben walked steadily forward.

"Good afternoon, my name is Ben Johnson, from North Carolina, I now have some land about a day west of here. Where y'all from?"

The men of the group spoke up and some were from both Carolinas, a couple from Virginia, one from Georgia. They all had met up at the crossing of the Tennessee River. They shared their harrowing crossing stories, and agreed they were blessed to have survived. The men continued talking about the land in the immediate area and if they were going to settle there. Ben recommended it. The heat of the afternoon was cooling as the sun went down and the stars came out. There was peace on the little hill comforting the families. It could feel like home to the newcomers.

"How are you doing, honey?" The women folk were getting to know the Johnson girls.

"We like it here just fine, but there aren't many people here, and Momma just died, so Daddy doesn't know what to do with us," offered Carol.

Deborah let the big sister do the talking; she remained on the shy side.

"You poor angels, well we all need help here. There are more little ones than we can keep up with. You girls think you can watch some children for us?"

Yes, ma'am." Carol made a quick reply and Deborah began eyeing all the running children in the camp.

Ben's search for support for his family was successful and more families followed him back to his land. They settled nearby and Cedar Grove was created with the Blackwells, Powers, Gateleys, Kirks, Smiths, Stanfords, James, and others whose offspring are now resting in the Potts cemetery.

The Johnsons thrived in that part of Tennessee. Ben, Jr. found a wife, and like his father, began reproducing like rabbits. His children stayed in the area and generations of Johnsons grew in the county. One branch of his seed had problems. Idiocy and crossed or miss matched eyes became frequent in that branch of children. Jimmy Patterson was to

discover a member of this branch when he found his wayward
dogs years later.

Pattersons

School was a priority. Katherine made sure Jimbo's homework got completed around his many chores about the farm. He had to learn organization, but until he did, his mother was there to guide him. He went to a school in a nearby town, which was made up of mostly city kids but had a few country kids and the bus route made its way to the Patterson farm.

The bus arrived each morning at the end of his long drive. It would come to a stop with a cloud of dust or splash of mud, depending on the weather. Jimbo would hop up the steps leaning against the weight of his stuffed book bag. He would cautiously look up to see the full bus of city kids and walk slowly down the aisle looking for a seat.

"Not here farm boy," the cute blond girl said.

"Keep moving redneck," came from a boy half his size.

"You smell," was the comment from the girl in the blue dress with white shoes.

Jimbo made his way to the back of the bus through a gauntlet of insults from the city kids and sat on the floor in front of the emergency exit door. It seemed that each day the insults grew worse. Once inside the big school house the torment increased with each city kid feeling the need to hurl an insult in his direction. Coming from the country was nothing to be ashamed of. When he got home that day, Jimbo took his confusion to the graveyard. He went directly to the Patterson section and talked to his grandparents and those who came before them. Once in a while when he was there talking to his ancestors, he noticed Caroline was visiting and talking to her aunt. They began to talk to each other and share their troubles with the living. He remembered his grandmother saying that his actions and behavior had a ripple effect back through history to reflect on all of his ancestors.

He decided to handle the insults with dignity and show that working the soil and being close to the Earth was an honorable life. He rose above the insults, and eventually the city kids were making room for him to sit on the bus. He invited his class out to the farm to demonstrate the equipment and show the animals.

The journal said:

Keep faith in the one in the mirror & the ONE within the one in the mirror.

He was the only one in his class to be able to drive a tractor. He also showed confidence in handling a horse. The city kids were immediately impressed. The insults stopped.

Jimbo and Caroline started a friendship. At times it seemed it was built on heartache, but then common ground emerged as they matured through the years. They learned to rely and trust each other. They became best friends at an early age. In his journal he read:

Friendship

Don't take this lightly, hold friendships seriously, almost sacred. Satan will place people in your life to tempt you. God will place people in your life to lead you to Him. Pay attention. A friendship is like being close to Jesus. Show others that you are worthy by being honest, dependable and trustworthy. The way to get a good friend is to be one.

The boy grew and the father relied on him more each day. Jimbo was a true partner holding up his end of the work. They both felt the loss of Emily's advice, but Katherine was filling that void daily.

The Pattersons were back as a solid family unit working, caring for the land as before the fire. The people and names had changed, but the commitment to the work and to this land remained. Jimbo was assurance that the Patterson gift from God would be cared for through another generation. The land prospered under Father and son.

Mother Earth.

Merle

He had been sitting there like he normally does for a long time without adding to the conversation or without really listening. His mind was years back when he took over his father's land and had to decide what to do with it. Three months earlier he had come by boat from Europe and from the killing fields. He and Sarah were going to marry and move into the homestead. The future was in front of him like a corn row. Long, straight and bright. Filled with promise. His father and those before him planted crops on the land and advised him to do the same. He remembered that day his family left and he was alone with the house and the land. It was a typical Southern summer day. Hot. Humid. The air was heavy with a threat of rain to come later. Heat waves radiated off the black dirt in the plowed, but not planted field. Sweat formed on him, air was tight. He took some steps out into *his* field to think. He didn't relish the idea of walking behind a mule and plow then planting a crop. He preferred to ride a horse and train one. There was more dignity to it in his mind. He stood there, like a tree. His legs were shoulder width apart, almost as if he were riding an imaginary horse. His arms loose at his sides. He looked down and saw black dirt and as his eyes accustomed to the brightness of the day he focused in the dirt a track that was indistinct, but taking shape in the dirt and in his mind. It soon became clear that he was looking at a horseshoe print in the dirt. Merle took this as a sign from God that he should go into the horse business in some way. And so he did. He was 25, about to marry, and had no money. He borrowed money from the bank using his land as collateral and started a horse training and stable business. He was good at it and word got around. Most folks in the area were farmers and did not have the time or horse skills, but still relied on horse transportation and relied on him. His business thrived until the automobile chugged its way out to the country replacing the horse. By that time he had repaid the bank, had his land back and was known in a wider area for his skills. Customers still came, but often from longer distances. Each new horse to train was a new challenge. He didn't "break" a horse like the traditional Western cowboys. His method was slower and gentler, and the end result was a better trained and reliable animal.

Merle rewound his memory tape to try to remember each horse he had handled over the years. He could identify so many. Some by markings, some by attitude, some by gait.

Now he must stand up and stretch the morning stiffness out. He feels the memory fog begin to clear from his eyes and current sounds and smells invade his senses. A young mother with her child and a gallon of milk protectively moves the child away. He realizes he has scared them, is embarrassed, and sits back down. The past is a friendlier place than the present. He sees himself brushing a bay mare so she shines and glistens in the morning sun. It isn't hot yet, so a good time to work a horse. The round pen exercises are complete, the edge has been taken off the mare and he will attempt to ride her today. They have established some trust. The mare knows he isn't a predator and he knows she won't purposely hurt him. He lets her smell the saddle blanket then rubs it on her to allay her fears. He gently places it on her back. Then he lets her smell the saddle and take a good look at it. She has been standing steady with the blanket on her back, has sniffed the saddle so he lifts it up onto the blanket. She reacts to the added weight on her back but doesn't panic. Merle is talking to her the entire time trying to calm her. He moves deliberately and with the confidence of the alpha animal in the relationship. Momentarily he wonders why he can talk to this bay mare and not to his wife. Then he realizes the bay responds and his wife doesn't. The saddle is on so he leads the mare around the corral slowly to get her used to the contraption on her back. She is calm. He is taking his time, talking to her, in a low voice. Merle leans some of his weight over the saddle ready to fall backwards if he has to. The mare is uncertain but unafraid still and tolerates the added weight and odd behavior. Then Merle, talking all the time, swings his long frame onto the saddle as easily as he can and sits quietly letting her digest what just happened. Merle can feel her quiver underneath him as she decides to either bolt, buck or relax and stand. Merle bets on good behavior and the mare relaxes as if in sync with his thoughts. They both stand still for a moment digesting a shared victory of trust. Merle smiles. His smile comes through the years and Bobbie wonders what he has been thinking. "Merle, are you good?" Booby inquires.

"Sure, I'm fine," Merle responds but he doesn't know who he is talking to.

Mattie

Mattie's story told through Caroline.

The walk up the concrete steps into the funeral home seemed to take forever. I felt the dread with each step. There was soft music droning on up at the top of the steps and inside. The funeral men opened up the big, church-like, wooden doors for us with sad smiles. It was a combination of "glad to see you, sorry someone you love is dead" kind of smile. They had professional sad smiles that came with a lot of practice. My sadness was new, and I couldn't smile. My mother moved over to where my aunt was lying. I had never been up close to a coffin before. It was a shiny slate gray, solid structure with red velvet inside. I moved closer.

The coffin, holding her, literally vibrated trying to hold on to her spirit. She reflected her usual calm, but her spirit was always on the lookout for something to do. Even in death. I know when they eventually close the lid that she will rest for eternity, but that spirit will find a way to soar.

I don't know where she ends and I begin. Her influence on me was so profound that I feel like she is living again through me. That was fine with me. I wasn't near as strong as she was. She taught me the lessons of life, but no, that is not quite right. She simply taught me life.

Now I have to decide where to go from here. My guiding light has gone out. I think that my life before her was too mundane. Destined to mediocrity. It would be a life with no waves, no conflicts, and no passion. She gave me a taste of passion. That is all it takes to change you forever.

I have to think through her eyes as to where my life will now lead. What would she do? And, oh how she would laugh at my crossroads. For her, there would be no indecision. There would be no wringing of the hands and looking for the safe road. She would risk safety, security, and the known, and jump down the road to the unknown, and laugh about it. Each cross-roads for her was yet another adventure.

The funeral home had few well wishers. Actually she outlived most of her old friends. The visitors were from the church, and they stopped by mainly out of a sense of duty. Not everyone liked my aunt. She was too much to understand.

The well wishers all spoke in hushed tones and paused to stare down into the coffin. They remarked how "natural" she looked and how much at peace she was. They didn't see what I saw, nor feel the vibrations rattling the coffin.

The funeral home had a lush, thick dark carpet. The curtains were drawn over the windows lest any sunlight would cheer the mourners. The dark, heavy fabrics swallowed up the sounds. What circulated in the air was a mixture of all the sounds of all the funerals that had been held in that room. The smell of despair was just as heavy mixing in the air. I looked down again at my aunt and felt her spirit raging against her death.

Mattie Ruth Herrick was scribbled on a birth certificate, soon to be chiseled in stone. 1895. That made her 96 when she died. She wanted so much to make it to 100. In fact, she never wanted to die at all. Her body finally gave into the years and forced the issue.

The funeral was quick by Southern standards. There was little speech making and only a prayer or two. No singing. The Methodist church echoed with the steps of the funeral men pushing her casket along on the wheeled cart up the aisle. Not many people there to muffle the footsteps. I jumped a bit when the hearse door was slammed. They didn't have to close the door that hard and disturb her.

The caravan to the cemetery was small. At the lead were a police car escort, the hearse, my parents, brother and I in a black limousine and three cars following us down the road. I had never been in a limo before. I thought a limo ride would be something to celebrate and have fun in. My first ride was supposed to be on a Prom night with all my friends. Laughing. There was crying going on in here now.

Cars along the road pulled over to let us pass. This was a Southern courtesy still practiced in West Tennessee. There was only one stoplight between us and the cemetery in Cedar Grove, and the cop let us breeze right through it.

There was a simple sign at the entrance stating we were at the Potts Cemetery. It looked like the P had fallen off and had been replaced at some point in time. Across from a barbed wire fence separating the cemetery were cows grazing in a pretty pasture of rolling hills. Flowers sprouted from vases scattered among the graves. Here and there flags were stuck in the vases to recognize the veterans who came home. It wasn't really a sad place until I saw the hole, a wound in the earth.

The funeral people try to spruce up the area by the hole by putting down Astroturf for us to walk on. I think they are afraid that some of the old church ladies might trip over the disturbed grass and fall. The bright green Astroturf didn't make the hole look any more inviting.

It was too pretty of a day for a sad funeral. The first signs of Fall were in the air. The sun was not as hot, the leaves were just beginning to lose their green and turn colors. The wind came from the north instead of the south. Across the road a horse lifted his head from grazing to sniff the smells brought in by the wind.

The men strained as they lifted Miss Mattie from the hearse. The wheeled cart didn't work over the grass, so they had to carry her. Now it was I who hoped one of them would fall and delay the inevitable. The casket must have been heavy. The men's knuckles were white with the strain and one guy's veins were bulging up around his neck by his collar. It was obvious that they had done this many times before. They made it to the opening of the hole and placed her coffin on some type of contraption that would lower her down. I was standing close to her and still could feel the uneasiness of her enclosed spirit.

The preacher said a few more words. It was more like a mumble of hard to distinguish words lost in the wind with a loud, solemn "Amen" at the end. I now understood the finality of that word. The contraption holding my great aunt squeaked and moved and the casket was making slow progress down into that hole. The church ladies became preoccupied with other thoughts and things and drifted back to their cars. My mother and I stood by the grave. Dad and my brother went over to talk with the funeral men and the preacher. The contraption stopped and I knew she was at the bottom.

My tears had been going on and off for the past few days. I thought they were all gone by now, but the sound of her casket bumping into the floor of the hole opened up more tears. They continued down my cheek and rolled off my chin as the sound of a shovel full of dirt banged off Miss Mattie. Mom had to leave and I knew she would be leaning up against my father by now. I couldn't move. Each shovel of dirt I felt, along with the spirit of my great aunt. The raging of that spirit didn't stop and I knew the earth around the grave would never settle.

I felt my father's big arm around my sagging shoulders.

"Come on Caroline. It is time we go home."

Now it was my turn to lean against him. He guided me back to the limousine, which was made blurry by my tears. Even with him close to me, I felt lost and alone. I don't remember the ride back to the church or even when we left the limo and got into our own car. Much of life was losing its significance.

As the sun went down that night, I thought about my aunt. It grew darker. In the night I worried about her spirit. How could a grave hold down the vibrancy that once roamed free? I prayed that God would welcome her home. Sleep came in fits.

Okolona, Mississippi was still recounting the Civil War. Most of the action occurred on porch steps and old rocking chairs creaking on porches. Every man from Okolona who had fought in that war was long dead, but stories were told and retold by those who had heard them originally from the knees of those old soldiers. There were few compliments for the Yankees, and most of the stories were sprinkled with a bunch of "only if" comments. The porches would be full of smoke from pipes and the sound of an occasional spit roughly aimed at a close bush.

"Mattie Ruth, see if Mr. Waller needs some more tea over there."

"Yes, ma'am."

Mattie was about ten years old and she had already heard these same stories told over and over again. Her job was to keep the flies off the pumpkin cake and keep the tea flowing. She drifted between the porch and big chair inside where she was reading another book on the big cities. Memphis, St. Louis, Chicago, New York. She let her mind drift across the country and imagined what it would be like to live in the excitement of those cities. Her father reminded her that most of those cities were full of Yankees and she should fear for her life. He also told her they all talked funny north of Memphis.

"Yes sir those Yankees came right down the main road there. They stopped near where the post office is now. Some even rested where Johnny's shop is down there," Mr. Waller was retelling his boring story. "Right then and there my uncle walked right up to a Yankee. 'Course he was a little feller then, but he was brave that day. He shook his finger at those Yankees and told them right then and there to get out of his town."

Mr. Waller would chuckle at that point in his story. That was always a sign for the other men to shake their heads and wonder at the bravery of that boy of yesterday. One of the men used the pause as a time to bang his pipe on the bottom of his heel to dislodge the burnt tobacco.

Mattie filled up the tea glasses and moved on back into the house. She had heard this story and witnessed this ritual far too many times. Another old story would follow this one and then another one. The heat of the afternoon would fade along with the stories. Soon the flies would be replaced by hungry mosquitoes. The men would drift home. It was the pattern of life in Okolona. Even at the tender age of ten, Mattie had grown bored with the place.

"Mattie, you go help your Daddy finish up out there, and the both of you come along for dinner," Mary Herrick called.

Mattie's mother was still young at 32, but life was hard and she looked like she was 52. Her face was already creased with lines that soon would become deep wrinkles. Her lines didn't follow a pattern caused by a lot of smiling and laughing in a lifetime. Her's were grim, and stuck in a pattern of sadness. It was a sadness brought on by four miscarriages and an abusive husband. Mattie was her "survivor," and she already knew that her daughter was dreaming beyond the borders of Okolona, Mississippi.

She approached him from behind as he tossed some hay to the mules and sole horse in the back of the lot. Mattie made a little scratchy noise with her feet so as not to spook the mules or her father. William Herrick didn't scare easily, but he didn't like surprises either.

"Hey there, Mattie. You going to help me out here?"

"Yes, sir. Momma wants us to finish up and come on to dinner."

"You go feed the dogs then and be sure you close that gate."

"Yes, sir."

Manners ran deep in the South. Mattie also knew that the less said, the better. Her father's moods changed faster than she was able to track, and sometimes she misjudged the mood while talking. At the age of ten, she already knew that the whiskey he drank made the moods change very fast, and a bottle was sitting on top of the fence post now.

The bottle was like a glass jar used for canning fruit, but it also held homemade whiskey pretty well. The Herricks didn't have the money to buy real bottled liquor, so Mattie's father relied on the friendship of the local moonshiner. She had taken a sip from one of those jars one time, and it took her breath away. The taste hurt all the way down and caused a fire in her belly. She could never figure out how her father gulped in full mouthfuls of the fiery stuff.

"Hey, quit standing around like one of them mules here and go feed those dogs." Her father's voice startled her from thinking about the white lightening contained in the fruit jar.

"Yes sir. I'm going now," Mattie said over her shoulder as she trotted off to the dogs.

Chores, school, old stories, feeding the dogs, being careful of her father. It was a pattern that Mattie saw in front of her for as long as she could see. Her future looked the same as if sighting down a long, straight, cotton row. From the perspective of a ten year old, that was a grim future.

Mattie Ruth was never sure when the impulse actually hit her to leave Okolona, Mississippi. It might have built up over the years so that when she was 17, she simply left. It might have happened as she slogged through the mud that night to feed the dogs.

Sleep was too hard the night after they buried her. I kept thinking about missing her. How could I go to school every day and not have her waiting for me to tell her of the day? The days would be insignificant if I couldn't tell her about all the details. The colors of the day, about which she and I talked would turn to gray. I wondered how other people got over missing someone.

"Caroline, what plans do you have today?" My mother was watching me closely, picking up on any little signals to show how I was coping.

"I dunno."

"I have some errands to run and a little bit of shopping to do. I could use some help." My mother was trying to be supportive.

I knew that. But, I wanted to be left alone. No, that isn't quite right. I wanted to be held, comforted and be safe again. My aunt would have known. My mother was too much of a rookie at comforting.

Blue green eyes smiling most of the time were dusted by blonde hair flying all about her face covering her dimples at times when the wind was blowing or when she was running. Mattie's face was as active as she was. All sorts of emotions and feelings flew across her face. She didn't—or couldn't—hide anything. Her face told the story of her feelings at that precise moment. The honesty of feeling burst out of her through her eyes and smiles. Unless the tears invaded. That happened sometimes when her father had too much from the fruit jar and went on the attack in the house. She cried for her mother.

At thirteen, she looked like Caroline looks now. Both had the eyes. Both had the shining blonde hair. The dimples were also part of the package that had survived another generation. The boys began to notice both of them at this age. Mattie liked the attention. Caroline wasn't so sure. Mattie could run faster. Caroline could read better. Both had potential.

Mattie walked around her house after dinner and after her chores. One of the dogs had run off that year and didn't return, so she had one fewer to feed. That was all right with her since that yellow dog had a bad attitude most of the time anyway. She didn't really have a purpose for her wandering, but she did pay attention to the house she was born in and had lived in for her now thirteen years. It needed paint. The well leaked above ground and made it muddy all the time. She could see where her father tried to patch the roof. It still leaked in a hard rain.

"Finding a roof leak is a damn hard thing to find. So you fix all around where you think it might be," he had told her.

He got angry at the weather when the wind blew the rain and some way or another a drip would form in the ceiling, always in a different spot.

The outhouse leaned to the left. You could see it. You could also feel the lean when you were inside of it. For the rest of her life, Mattie leaned a bit to her right to level herself when she used the toilet.

Circling the house for the second time she found herself not looking at the house but looking for reasons to be there. The only one she could come up with is that she was only thirteen with no way to support herself. The frustration was building. Okolona was not in her future, but at her age the future was coming at her in slow motion. Mattie wanted some action. She returned to her picture books and imagined Paris. She read by candlelight. Electricity was still finding its way to Mississippi out in the country. With no radio or television or internet, Mattie listened to her father's snoring in the background. His breathing was abrupt, loud and even angry in his sleep. She wondered how her mother ever got any rest. Maybe the snoring was the cause of the dark circles under her mother's eyes.

More time was spent with the white lightning in the fruit jar than farming. Mattie's father was at war with himself. His internal skirmishes would not be the fodder for future conversations on porches recounting glorious battles. William Herrick was having his own, personal Civil War. And, just like the Old South, this was one that couldn't be won.

There was collateral damage just like in all wars. Mattie and her mother were the primary targets, but the mules got their share of abuse too. It was as if Mattie's father expected the mules to plow the fields all by themselves. He beat them every day as the fields grew only weeds. All of the dogs had already run off. Even the house suffered. One rainy night another drip formed on the ceiling, which became the focus of his daily wrath. And with a wavering focus, he shot the drip with his 12 gauge shot gun. The living room now had a large washtub on the floor catching the rainwater.

I was learning the finality of death. Mom and Dad were being careful around me. My brother was even being nice to me. The void, the hole in me still was huge. I knew time would help fill it in, but I was early in this grieving process and still hurt. I found myself spending hours thinking about her. My aunt was too important to me and she left too early.

Her room still smelled like her. Mom hadn't done anything with the room and it looked just like it did when Aunt Mattie was alive and living with us. I spent time sitting in the rocker that she had next to her bed. I would rock and think about our conversations. The squeak of the rocking chair used to mingle with our laughter. It was a happy time. Now the rocker's sound is more like a moan.

I found myself looking through her things. Mom said it was OK for me to do that and to keep whatever I wanted. Her closet had a mixture of her daily clothes. They looked like what an old person would wear. A trunk in the attic held clothes from her earlier life. I had used some of those dresses for play and even for Halloween costumes. The clothes in her closet brought back familiar smells.

She had some jewelry, but most of it was not really expensive. I had also used some of her jewelry when I played dress-up. Aunt Mattie didn't care. Now the old jewelry looked priceless to me. I handled each piece with gentle care.

In the back of her closet was a small trunk. I always thought it held more old clothes and had never opened it. Today I pulled it out to the front of the closet so the light would help me find the latches. The trunk was a combination of old leather and wood fixed together to hold whatever was inside. I knew you couldn't buy a trunk like this new. No one made trunks like this any more.

The latches were stuck with time and grit, but eventually eased and the top of the trunk creaked open. Inside was a combination of things that made up a life. There were old black and white picture books of Paris, New York, San Francisco and London. A few photos of smiling young men were tucked in a corner. More photos of a young Mattie were sprinkled throughout the trunk. I thought she was a beautiful woman at all her ages.

There were letters. The letters were tied with a string and the entire pack had yellowed with age. Then there was her diary. It was a journal of sorts. A hardbound booklet with empty pages that now contained the thoughts of a young woman. Her handwriting was as beautiful as she was.

I felt a rush of excitement discovering this treasure from my aunt. At the same time I felt guilty or more like I was intruding into her private affairs. Grief, guilt and excitement make up for a strange combination. Mainly I was confused.

Today I decided to put everything back in its proper place, close the lid and push the trunk back into the darkness of the closet. Tomorrow I'll know more what to do.

That night I kept thinking of what I might find in her journal and in those letters. Who were those young men in the fading black and white photos? I knew then that my pathway to living past my grief was to be found inside the darkness of that old trunk. I decided to let the light in on the contents, and maybe the light would shine in on me at the same time.

"Mattie Ruth."

The sound was hollow. William Herrick continued his downward spiral. He spent all his time with the fruit jars, and the mules were left to wander the fields that they were supposed to be plowing.

She ignored the calling of her name.

The Herrick household had moved from bad to worse. Tragedy was only around the corner, but then, so too, was her life. Quietly she gathered her few things, peeked in at her sleeping mother, and left. She had memories to make, and a trunk to fill.

Caroline saw the first diary entry, which was very short and simple:

"Today I left home. I'll miss Momma, but not Poppa. Time to live."

Caroline followed Mattie from Mississippi to Georgia where she lived and worked as a waitress for several years then on to New York City through her journal and a few early letters. She noticed the excitement in Mattie and the concern in her mother wanting her child to return. The train tickets were saved in the trunk next to the journal.

Mattie became a Red Cross volunteer during World War II and spent time with injured soldiers as they returned from Europe through New York City. Eddie was one of those injured boys and they became friends. The diary quickly related how the friendship grew to her first love. Mattie was new to these emotions and probably moved too quickly to marriage, and her diary entries were almost giddy with her excitement. Apparently the advice from her mother's letters was largely ignored concerning men. Mattie and Eddie were married and Caroline, through the years, could tell a mistake had been made.

The diary entries moved from the excitement of a new love to the sadness of a marriage falling apart. She spoke of recoiling from his touch and feeling stress as she entered their house and remembered the fear of her mother. The marriage ended in divorce and Mattie was back at her best, being free. Then there was another letter that caught Caroline's eye. It was in a neat and steady hand writing.

"Dear Mattie, I must be going. Thank you for helping me during my recovery. Your daily cheerfulness made learning to walk again much easier. That German bullet in my leg did some damage, but they say I'll be good as new very soon. You are made for the city and adventure. I am made for the country and the steady, quiet life. We talked about being a couple, but I don't think it would work out. You are worried about being a little older than I am, but my concern is that we are too different in temperaments. We want different things in life. I'm afraid I would eventually bore you as a farmer with a love of the land while you love the lights and the hustle and bustle of the city. I best get back to Tennessee and look for land where my family came from in a tiny place called Cedar Grove.

Take Care of yourself,
James Patterson.

Rev. John Taylor

John Taylor, grew up in the windy plains and flint hills of Kansas, went to Kansas Wesleyan University in Salina, Kansas where the interest to be a Methodist minister was ignited. The campus was an oasis in the plains with green grass and an abundance of big lush trees full of squirrels. There weren't that many trees from where he grew up. Green trees and a love for the Lord became his passions. That led to his ordination as a Methodist minister and eventually to a small church in Cedar Grove, Tennessee. The church was about a quarter mile down the highway from Lilly's general store. It had a circle drive so folks could be dropped off at the front steps of the building. A cemetery was off to the right where past church members gathered. The church had an abundance of stained glass windows, but the woods, full of trees, behind the church is what first drew Rev. Taylor's attention when he came for a visit.

He was a natural Southerner who just had to learn the language and the customs. That didn't take long, and he soon fit in like he had been there for generations. John Taylor was tall, with dark brown eyes and hair. He looked like a smoother version of Abe Lincoln. His voice was deep and clear, which was good for preaching.

"Good morning brothers and sisters, so nice to see y'all here today. The Lord has been good to us this

Spring blessing us with rain and sunshine. I see your crops bursting from the ground and pray for a good harvest this year for you," he began.

Do you notice what you see on television or in the news even on the internet if you know how to use a computer? All the "stuff" people are trying to sell us. Buy this, get that. Then you will be happy. NO! Y'all don't be fooled. Whenever you desire something too much, you begin to grow dissatisfied with yourself. Then when you get that new frivolous "thing" are you really happier or do you crave the next new thing? Those who are full of pride are never contented. Those who are humble in spirit are the ones who live in peace. When you are too full of yourself you leave no room for God in your life. You must die to yourself, to your pride, and open your heart and live for Christ. Beware of Satan offering frivolous, temporary things; these prideful things take your attention to you and away from our Savior.

Say Amen.

Rev. Taylor paused for a while and let the silence help the message soak in. The choir took over and the church filled with music. Rev. Taylor switched his notes preparing for what he called round two of the morning.

Remember the Bible passage of Jesus and the woman caught in adultery? You probably remember the line such as "who among you is without sin, cast the first stone." Or when He told the woman "Go and sin no more." But this passage in John 8: 1-11 intrigues me in another way. The Scribes and Pharisees come with this woman and judgment on their minds. They are ready to stone this woman, and are using the occasion to test Jesus' knowledge of the Law. As they begin to tell Him of her adultery, Jesus bends down and writes something in the dirt without responding. The accusers keep on ranting, and then Jesus bends down and writes some more. Then, a funny thing happens. The accusers begin to drift off leaving the woman and Jesus alone. He asks her where did they go? She doesn't know. He tells her to go and sin no more. We don't know, and the Bible never tells us what Jesus wrote in the dirt that day. My theory is that Jesus, knowing what is in our hearts, wrote the names of those elders and the sin or sins next to their names. He didn't have to say a word. The elders saw their name and what was written and knew they were not without sin and therefore not worthy to cast a stone, and left the scene. We don't know that detail in the story, but I believe that Jesus does know what is in our hearts. Go and sin no more.

Say Amen.

The Rev. John Taylor became part of the fabric of Cedar Grove. He Baptized, Married, buried, and counseled his flock and other families of the area. Rev. Taylor was the "go to" guy with any religious question or theological issue. He also was the center of the charitable arm of the community. Any family on hard times was on his list, and travelers along HWY 70, "the Broadway of America," got assistance if needed.

He looked up from his desk as the church secretary knocked on his office door.

"Pastor, there is a young traveler in the sanctuary. I think he might need you," she said.

"Thank you Martha, tell him I'll be right there and please see if he is hungry or thirsty," replied Taylor.

Rev. Taylor looked into the church's sanctuary and saw a man in his twenties with a dirty backpack sitting in a front pew with his head down in his hands.

"Good morning young man, my name is Reverend Taylor looks like you are a traveler on our Broadway of America. Are you OK?" He extended his hand in welcome.

"Good morning Reverend, my name is Kirk Phillips, I'm from Memphis on my way to maybe Indianapolis or I don't know. Somewhere."

"Son, you look troubled. Are you hungry? What do you need?"

"Reverend, I could use some food, but I really need a miracle. I'm going to go to hell I know it."

"Kirk, let's get some food into you, then let's you and me talk. Hell is serious business."

The two walked down the road to Lilly's store and the boy ate his fill on the church's credit, then they walked back, but John Taylor guided the boy to a set of benches just inside the woods behind the church.

"This is my favorite quiet spot. It seems big problems get smaller here," Taylor said.

"I appreciate the food, Reverend." Replied Kirk.

"Now tell me what troubles you, Son. Why do you think you are going to Hell?"

"I have sinned. Sinned real bad."

"Kirk we are all sinners. Running from your sin won't fix it though and I know you can't run from God. Jesus came here to take all of our sins into him. He died for us. God loves you just as your imperfect self. You aren't alone. You never have been alone. God has always been with you."

"But Preacher man, I killed someone. That is against the Ten Commandments, you go to Hell for that. But he was hitting my momma so hard, I had to stop him, then he didn't move and I ran. I've been running ever since," the young man had a hard time getting his story out and he sobbed out the last part.

"Are you sure you killed this person? Maybe you just knocked him out and ran off before you knew," suggested Taylor.

"I don't know, and it was dark, but I think I killed him."

"Son, let's know for sure so you can stop all this running. Sooner or later you will get caught anyway. It will be better for you to contact the law first. I'll go with you."

"Thank you Reverend, but I don't want to trouble you. I can contact the law myself."

"We can call them from the church, and I bet you get a free ride back to Memphis," Taylor tried a light joke, but got only a wry smile for the effort.

Hours later the police car was in the front drive waiting for its passenger. "Remember Kirk, God is always with you everywhere you go. I'll be praying for you and checking up on you too."

Prayer

"Good-bye Reverend and thank you. I'll come by to see you again."

Then he was gone.

"Yes Martha, what is it?"

"The Williams family called to ask if you would go over to their house for a visit. Old Mrs. Goodwell is ailing and she asked for you."

The Williams' had lived in Cedar Grove for several generations. Mrs. Goodwell and her husband once ran a general store similar to Lilly's years ago. Her daughter and grandsons lived next door and her great grand daughter was close by. She and the grandsons maintained Potts Cemetery to the highest standards, and had the courage to face down the bad intentions of Bud from time to time. If there was a mayor or "Queen" of Cedar Grove, Mrs. Goodwell was it, but in her late 80's she was slowing and ailing now. She didn't have much time left, and knew it.

Mrs. Williams, the daughter, opened the door. "Thank you Reverend Taylor for coming over. Momma has been asking for you."

"Good afternoon Peggy, I'm happy to look in on one of my favorite church members. Your mother was one of the first to welcome me here when I was appointed to the church. We have been friends for a long time."

"Momma is resting in her room. I'll take you to her. Do you want some tea?"

"No thank you, I'm fine for now. Let's go see your mother."

In a semi-darkened room lay the old woman.

"Sister, how are you today," asked Taylor?

"Oh Pastor, so kind of you to look in on me. I'm not up to my perky self, you know," she replied.

"We both are slowing down a bit," he said as he picked up her wrinkled hand and sat beside her.

"You are still a Spring chicken, you don't know what old is yet, preacher man."

"When I get there, I hope to do it with the grace I see in you though," he went on.

"Reverend, I'm scared. I don't tell Peggy because I don't want to worry her. Do you know what lies beyond this world," she asked?

Stroking her old hand, he said, "No ma'am, I don't think any of us living have had much of a look into the beyond."

"I'm scared. It seems cold and dark to me."

"Sister, my view is the opposite. I see light, the warm light of God welcoming us to his home for all of eternity. I see the saints, my parents, my little sister who died when she was eleven and my brother who was killed in the military. I see my grandparents, and us all together as a family again. It is a warm bright light glow of love. I see Jesus."

Thank you Reverend, that changes everything. I'll think about that for awhile. Mrs. Goodwell drifted off to sleep with a smile on her lips, happy with her dreams of Jesus.

A few weeks later Reverend Taylor officiated at the burial of Mrs. Goodwell at the Potts Cemetery. The grandsons still maintain it in perfect condition and take special care of her plot.

Pattersons

"You should go out on a date sometime, go find a pretty girl," Katherine advised son.

"I am way too busy to waste time on a girl, besides most city girls aren't made out for farm life and don't understand it," countered Jimbo.

Briefly he thought of his friend, Caroline, but didn't see her as dating material. The last time he saw Caroline was a late afternoon when they both were visiting the cemetery.

"Hi Caroline, visiting Aunt Mattie?" He inquired.

"Yes, after school my mother brought me out here for a while before supper. I guess you are here to visit your grandparents?" she responded.

"No, I was walking between pastures and just came by for a quick hello when I saw you over here. I have to get home. Mom wants me to do some chores before our supper. See you around. Bye."

"Bye."

Caroline enjoyed her privacy in the cemetery with her thoughts and her aunt. The sun was going down and the cemetery grew dark quickly under the trees. She got up to stretch her legs and read the names on the graves nearby. It was very quiet there, and as she walked she began to hear a voice, then others, almost like wind rustling the leaves. As she walked amongst the graves the voices became more distinct:

"*Regret, Regret, Regret.*"

Is what she heard from one grave to the next. She went to her aunt's grave and heard no regrets. Caroline made a promise to herself to live a life of no regrets right then.

Meanwhile Jimbo skipped up on the porch to help his father with the latest chore.

"Hold it level," father and son working on a front porch project.

"Dad, This swing looks just like the one Grandmother and Grandpa had at the old house," Jimbo observed.

"Yes, it is exactly like the old one. Both were made by the Mennonite families down the road there. They make the best porch swings. Always have," replied Jim.

Katherine came out to inspect the work of her men folk. She tested the seat with her hands, and then sat on the swing. Jim sat down on her right; Jimbo occupied the space on her left. Surrounded by the Patterson men, Katherine felt secure. She looked off the porch out onto the land,

Mother Earth, closed her eyes and offered a *prayer* of thanksgiving.

M&M

Mark and Melinda were a couple. They worked

hard. He did odd jobs for a number of the famers and families around Cedar Grove since the poor economy laid him off his good job. Melinda did the same. Mark was all muscle. He wasn't tall, but he did a man's work all day long every day. He had the ability to look at a mechanical or farm problem and figure out a solution. He wasn't book smart, but he was brilliant where needed in the field or shop.

Melinda was pretty. It started with her blue eyes. She had dark, black, long hair that set off those eyes and her smile. Long legs and a good figure turned heads when she walked into a restaurant or a store. Mark noticed the looks, but was secure in their relationship so wasn't jealous.

Bud hired Mark to help him do some work around his shop. Melinda happened to be in Mark's truck that first day, and Bud noticed her. Bud then hired Melinda to clean up his shop one evening after Mark had left for the day. As Melinda was mopping the floor, Bud came up behind her and she felt hands groping her all over. Melinda was strong in her own right. She pushed Bud away and screamed at him. This startled him enough to cause him to leave.

"Mark he touched me all over and I had to push him off of me,"

Melinda always told Mark everything.

"That SOB." Mark was working into a rage.

"Calm down. I handled it," she said.

"I'm going to talk to him in the morning when I see him. He won't try that stunt again."

Mark pulled his old pickup next to Bud's workshop. One of the farm hands was already there with Bo, the co-op man, taking an order. Bud was drinking coffee and stood up as Mark walked in the door.

"Bud, Melinda told me what you did last night. You keep your stinking hands off her."

"Mark she lied. She wanted me anyway," Bud replied.

Mark took a few steps in Bud's direction. Bud put down his coffee cup, and picked up his long hunting knife off the table. Pointing it at Mark he said,

"Get back."

Bud lunged at Mark with the knife, but Mark was quick and strong. He dodged the knife. Bud came at him again, but harder this time. He lunged at Mark and screamed hoping to scare him. Mark grabbed Bud's wrist, turned the knife as Bud stumbled into his own weapon. Bud would die that night from the knife wound, and it was good for Mark that he had two eyewitnesses to the event that would keep him clear of the law. There were no tears shed in Cedar Grove for Bud. Bud, the ill wind, was gone.

Emails

Jim also leased land from a city man who had recently moved to that part of the country. The city man had built a house on his property, bought a few horses and leased his pastures to Jim. The following are emails sent after an ill-fated horse ride on this property:

#1

Family and Friends, as Mary repeatedly tells me, "This isn't funny."

Yesterday was a beautiful Fall day, sunny, warm, and perfect to go horseback riding on the farm. The trees are changing colors, grass green, the land beckoned. Some friends (witnesses) were with us. We saddled up, headed off.

Mary & I weren't quite like Roy Rogers and Dale Evans, but I thought she was about to sing. Halfway into this wonderful ride Mary fell off her horse. At first she said she was dead. She later modified it to "every bone in my body is broken." There was no blood, but there was something you could roughly classify as "yelping." For those of you that know us, you have run to the ending of the story and know it is my fault. Yes, my fault she fell off the damn horse. Apparently "John didn't put the saddle on right." (I didn't do it on purpose.) So, with a little effort and a big front-end loader, we got her vertical again. Now she thinks it might be ribs. At one point her fingers were poised over her phone at 911 and the helicopter rescue service. (Yes, we are far out in the country) After some home made medicine (wine and pills), she decided to give it a day to see if she would live through the night. She did, and awoke her usual sunny self, but still in pain and still remembered it was my fault. Today I get a new saddle cinch. The rest of the day I will be playing nurse, serving every need and whim. Apparently Mary did not read the sign in the barn written in BIG letters, "ride at your own risk"!

ding--ding #2

Family & Friends. An update is in order. Mary says she is feeling better. (Hard to tell attitude wise). We have this little bell (made by the devil) that she rings when she "really needs" something. It goes ding-ding. Words. Have you noticed how they don't mean the same thing? Take patient and being patient. There is not a patient patient in my experience. Ding-ding.

I do not intend to take Mary's riding accident (my fault) and her recovery (my job) into a mini-series, but it does have potential.

Early this morning I took the devil's bell out to see if it could float in our pond. I tossed it about 150 yards (could be a world record). It doesn't. (Float, that is.)

I know Mary is feeling better. There is less screaming. I'm going to spend part of the day shopping for one of those cute little white nurses' uniforms.

bang—bang #3

Family & Friends

We finally went to get X-rayed. Poor Mary. Good news/bad news.

Bad news is that "there are multiple fractures between ribs 4 & 9 on the left side". Good news is that they gave her some nifty pain pills and a pain shot that seemed to have worked. Now we must decide to either use or sell the pills. (joke)

Using my vast medical knowledge, I offered information: "Honey (note the endearment). You are older and your bones are more brittle and apt to break."

Her response was short, but specific: "Get the gun, put 2 bullets in it, go to the barn, shoot that damn horse, then shoot yourself."

I think she must be feeling better. Her old, cheerful, friendly, Dale Evan's self is re emerging.

Mary has something to say #4

Mary: Don't encourage him. This could go on for months. He ain't raight......

John here: I don't understand what she means, but there could be more to the story.

the rest of the story #5

Family & Friends:

Due to my caring, nurturing (and answering that damn bell), I think Mary is feeling better. Lately I have: cooked, cleaned, laundered, mowed, painted the house (inside and out) cleaned the gutters, changed all the air filters, held a garage sale, and turned her pillows to make her "comfy."

There is a "rest of the story" that mere modesty has held me back from sharing, but it is time for you to hear the full story of that fateful day when Roy & Dale went riding.

Mary was doing just fine (she made me say that). Then the saddle slipped (my fault) "John didn't put the saddle on right." The horse stepped one way sprightly, she went the other way almost gracefully and the ground came up quickly. As she was on the ground claiming that she was dead, the horse was prancing around her prone body. I leapt from my steed, rushed to her side, grabbed the reins of her (now wild) horse and kept the horse from stomping on her. From my right, I noticed Indians coming over the hill. Holding the wild horse with one hand, trying not to step on Mary "yelping" on the ground, I fought off the Indians with my one free hand.

As they turned tail to run back to the woods, I

noticed creeping out of the bush a bear, mountain lion, and a rabid coon. Using a page out of Davy Crockett's book, I "stared down that bar." He lowered his head, got back down on all four feet and lumbered back into the bushes. The mountain lion and rabid coon conferred for a moment, and must have decided that if big old bear didn't want any part of me, then they better show some forest judgment too.

So, they lowered their tails, turned and followed the bear back to the bush. I looked around for more danger. Remembering Mary on the ground, I tried to lift her with my one hand (remember I'm holding a wild horse in the other). Well, as petite as Mary is, I couldn't get her up one-handed. (thus the need for the front-end loader of my tractor).

Now she is having her second cup of coffee (not too hot, not too cold---just right), breakfast and the pain pills (mixed with 2 bottles of wine last night) seem to have a calming effect. I plan to wash and wax her car today before I get all the flowerbeds and garden ready for the winter.

Caroline

She liked the country and her visits to Cedar Grove. School kept her busy and soon she was off to college at

Tulane in New Orleans. It was a new experience and a new adventure, which she faced alone and wished she could share with her aunt Mattie. Caroline had dated a little in college, but no one seemed to become special. The boys just didn't have the "substance" or character she wanted and was looking for. Those boys came and went after a few dates. She often worried if anyone could measure up to her high standards, and these college boys seemed to be too "soft" and not capable of really taking care of her.

Like many college students, Caroline didn't have much of a clue or direction as to what to do upon graduation. She gave her future a lot of thought, and found her mind drifting back to Aunt Mattie's old trunk in the closet with the brochures of far away cities. One night she decided to follow Mattie's dreams and visit those cities. In some way she felt that she would complete Mattie's girlhood dreams, and maybe find a direction in her own life in the process. She had already seen Memphis and Nashville so Chicago was her first target with New York City and maybe San Francisco later. Paris was out of her budget for the time being. Caroline had a Honda Civic, which got decent gas mileage and had a good radio in it. One day she loaded it with her luggage, filled up with gas, checked tires and oil like her father always advised and headed north from New Orleans, the Crescent city. It seemed easy, stay on hwy

55 going north for a long time then turn right in St. Louis to Chicago. She tooted her horn to acknowledge Memphis as she passed, and briefly thought of Cedar Grove and Jimbo 90 miles to the East.

Caroline saw the skyscrapers in the distance first as she approached Chicago. The two-lane highway had already expanded to four lanes and soon to be six. She preferred the no traffic of Cedar Grove to the fast, heavy traffic of Chicago, but eventually she found her way downtown and a parking garage with those going to work for the day. She blended in with the worker bees and emerged on the sidewalk noting some green space across the street, which she gravitated over to. The little park fronted Lake Michigan, and it was a good place to sit on a bench, rest, and plan her next move. She didn't know anyone in Chicago, and didn't want to waste her dwindling money on an expensive hotel. She decided to walk around downtown awhile, let rush hour get over then continue on to New York. She saw where people lived in condominiums along Front Street with pretty views of the Lake, and understood that most people commuted in to work, but lived out in the suburbs miles away. New Orleans was a city, but nothing like what she was experiencing in Chicago. This place was noisy, way too many people, and BIG. Cedar Grove looked very inviting right now. But she learned that Chicago wasn't all that big when she compared it to New York City.

New York was all hustle and bustle, noise, and the number of jostling people was just too much for her comfort level. Caroline looked up in the air from sidewalk level to the towering buildings all steel and glass. She thought for a moment of the walks she used to have in the country looking up at the towering oak trees. She thought, "This is the difference between Man and God." Her preference was for the trees. She also didn't like how many of the men looked at her. She thought it was lustful leering and it made her uncomfortable. She did try out the subways and visited the tourist spots to be sure she had a full experience, but she was ready to leave after a few days in the Big Apple. Caroline drove as far as Nashville to catch a plane to San Francisco and leave her car in Tennessee.

San Francisco was easier, more laid back. It was still a big city, but not as hectic as New York or Chicago. The taxi took her from the airport into the city and she walked around the next day to see Fisherman's Warf, and spend time near the Golden Gate Bridge. She could see Alcatraz and Coit Tower. She also walked around China town and up and down some of the big hills of the city. Near the end of the day she got a glass of wine and sat on a bench on the beach and gathered her thoughts. The ocean actually reminded her of Lake Michigan.

Caroline had traveled many miles from New

Orleans to Chicago to New York City to San Francisco. Her adventures so far did bring a few conclusions for her. She was weary of traveling for now, and wanted to go home. She was not a fan of big cities and truly preferred the quiet pace of the country life. She was lonely.

Billy Berkley and Rev. Taylor

Lilly's store was the gathering place for farmers taking a coffee break and a shopping place for folks who needed little items and didn't want to drive all the way into town for them. It was also a meeting place for the Rev. Taylor and Billy Berkley to discuss spiritual matters. Rev. Taylor often tried out a sermon idea on Billy before he developed it for his flock.

"Billy, I'm thinking about developing a sermon on the Gospel Mark 4:35 when Jesus calms the storm in the sea so the boat he and his disciples are in does not capsize. What do you think is the meaning of that story?" Merle was close by but deep in his own world of the past. He was concentrating but not of things in the present.

"Rev. that story is also in Matthew and Luke, the Synoptic Gospels. My thoughts are that the storm represents "life." We all are tossed around by the storms of life threatening to drown us, but our faith and trust in Jesus will calm these storms and everything will be all right. Jesus even chastised his disciples in the boat by saying "Ye of little faith." The theme of your sermon should be "Trust in Jesus." Billy was rubbing his index finger against his thumb as he talked to push his words out.

"Thank you Billy, that helps clarify my thoughts," replied Taylor.

A few days later Rev. Taylor poured some hot coffee into Billy's mug.

"Billy, a church member asked me yesterday how does a person learn the faith?" How would you respond to that question?"

"Reverend, there is no simple, one size fits all answer for that one. St. Paul got knocked off his horse by Jesus who then talked to him. Paul got his faith all at once. I think, for most people, it is a *journey* and not an event. I think faith is a gift from God, but that you must take the steps necessary to be open to accept the gift. Those steps would be prayer, reading the Bible, spending time in the quiet presence of God and, over time, your gift and faith will grow. For me, I had little faith and little interest. Then the scaffolding fell. I had plenty of time in the hospital to think and I knew that I couldn't do everything by myself like I had been doing. I needed to 'give up' so to speak and learn to trust God. It took me quite a while to 'let go and let God.' But, now I'm a much better person. It just was hard to change a lifetime of relying on myself, and not trusting in God. There is wisdom in the saying of 'die to yourself and live in Christ.' My faith journey included prayer, lots of scripture reading and studying, but most of all, the quiet time, like a hermit, being in the presence of the Lord and emptying myself of myself and welcoming the Lord in. As time went on, this became natural and it felt like God's will for me." Billy said as he rubbed his fingers together.

"Or you could quote this: 'Faith is confident assurance concerning what we hope for, and conviction about things we do not see.' (Heb 11:1)."

"Thank you again Billy, I'll share that with this person and see if we can help him on his faith journey," Taylor said.

Later that day.

"OK, Billy, this is a tough one. Explain the Body, Soul, and Spirit. What's the difference among the three?" asked Rev. Taylor.

"I'll need to think about that a little bit. Today I'm mowing, and I'll contemplate on your question and offer you an answer tomorrow," replied Billy the philosopher.

The next day, with the farmers at one end of the long table, Merle had been standing for a long time quietly looking out a window. Rev. Taylor and Billy huddled quietly at the other end the answer was forthcoming.

"I'm not sure this is right. You may want to check with your theologian experts, but my thoughts are that the Body is simply our physical shells. 'Dust to dust.' The other two are more complicated. The Soul is like what John Locke, the English philosopher, mentioned as 'Tabla Rosa' or a Blank Tablet which we write our life's experiences on every day. It could also be our conscience. It is connected to the Body and dies with the Body. The Spirit is 'eternal.' It is the 'breath' that God breathed into Adam and into 'everyman.' As Body and Soul dies, the Spirit goes to heaven. When Jesus comes again to gather all men and souls then the Body, Soul and Spirit will be united again in heaven.

Another angle you might research is one suggested from my good friend, Jim, who is now a deacon. He started out as a bouncer in a bar up in a mountain overlooking Denver. He might have found religion in the sparse air there or in the Viet Nam jungles where he fought and served our country. Anyway, Jim says to read St. John of the Cross to find your body, soul, spirit answer. That approach is probably better than my attempt. Jim might have been quoting someone else, but one of his favorite sayings is, "we are spiritual be-ings having a human existence."

"Billy, you are getting pretty deep for a handyman. Maybe that big bump on your head gave you insight beyond the university theologians. Thank you for your thoughts." Said Taylor. "The only thing is that I'm afraid it is over the heads of my congregation," continued Taylor.

"One thing that won't be over their heads and is basic, is love. God is Love. Tell them that love is our authentic and true selves, and we spend too much time covering up "us" with stuff and junk like worry, anxiety, meaningless work, useless possessions, and shallow re-lationships. We should spend time stripping ourselves back down to our essence where we will find love, and where we will find God, and He will find us.

We crowd out love and God with this 'stuff and junk.' This is another time to remind folks to "die to themselves and live in Christ," Billy said.

"The New Testament is a love story," added Taylor.

Merle, looking out the window could see years ago a pretty dark pony that he had specially trained for Sarah. He had selected the right horse and spent extra time training it. He made sure the pony was safe with the right manners and one day brought the gelding up to the house to present to her. She didn't come to the door. He called again. She was gone and he never saw her again. Some folks say she went to Jackson and took a train from there. He took the trained horse to a big pasture that bordered woods and had no fences all the way to the Tennessee River and let him go. He can see the flick of its tail and the tentative search for freedom then the race towards it; then both Sarah and this horse were gone forever.

"Billy what makes you so wise?" Rev. Taylor wanted to know.

"I don't see myself as wise at all. I do try to practice less 'doing' and more 'being.' I might be like a present day Desert Father. The original ones tried to imitate Jesus by going out to the desert as hermits, away from the hustle and bustle of the first and fourth century madness and contemplate on the life of Christ. St. Anthony was one of the early ones to do this. I try to separate myself from the hustle and bustle of this century's madness and be a hermit contemplating on the life of Christ. Instead of a desert, I do my thinking in the woods of Cedar Grove. You can have clarity of thought when you practice less 'doing and more being.' A life imitating Christ ain't bad either," Replied Billy.

"Billy, you are amazing. I don't understand how you think so deeply about all these topics. What makes you tick?" Rev. Taylor was impressed a redneck from Cedar Grove was teaching him more than all his professors at Kansas Wesleyan University.

"Reverend. I think we are all made to be holy. We are created in His image. God breathed the Holy Spirit into each of us. God dwells inside each of us. He has a plan for each of us. Our job is to get out of the way and listen for the voice of God guiding us to this plan, then structure our lives to it. That's the hard part. Most of us have our own plans we hang on to so tightly, and can't trust God enough to let go. Some people throughout history were better at hearing His voice, letting go, and aligning their lives with His will. We call those people saints. Then there is Jesus. He probably most perfectly aligned His will with that of the Father's. My goal is to simply listen. The rest I trust to God," replied Billy.

"I should have you preaching every Sunday at the church. I think your message is more powerful than mine. "Billy, how do you explain God?" was Taylor's next question.

"Reverend, I think the closer you get to know God, the less you are able to use words to describe Him. This is a very personal journey and a very personal relation-ship that words are just too frivolous to use, so silence is the best course."

Billy, who are you?" asked Taylor.

"Now that's a deep question Reverend. Most of us live a shadow of our true selves. We spend our energy polishing this mask of whom we present to the world and to the mirror. Our energy is to live up to the expectations of others and to the imagined greatness in others. It is a world of illusions. Our true selves get lost in the illusions we so carefully build and nurture. We have a world of pseudo identities running around and the more we work to make of ourselves the more we actually cease to exist."

"Billy, I need to think about that some. It might be over my head," replied Taylor.

"It is a basic concept, preacher man. The idea is to die to yourself, the false, worldly self and rise in Christ, your true, Godly inward self, " Billy replied hitching up his overalls.

In the background you could hear the farmers complain about cotton prices, politics in Washington and the weather. Mothers purchased milk and bread, and life moved on in Cedar Grove as theology was discussed over hot coffee at Lilly's store.

Merle relives another chapter of his life quietly.

Rev. Taylor & Billy Berkley continued

Taylor and Billy decided to walk up to the church

and continue their discussion on the bench in the woods behind the church where it was quieter.

"Billy I need help in creating a very short sermon, and I tend to give long ones. What would you do?" asked the Reverend Taylor.

After a pause, Billy replied.

"God is a mystery. We can't begin to comprehend Him with the limited human mind. So, have Faith. Imitate Christ. Love your neighbor. Amen.

Or you could try this: I was in love with a woman once. I spent every minute thinking of ways to make her happy.... Finding ways to spend more time with her. Shouldn't we love God with that same kind of energy and intensity? Amen."

Billy was almost rubbing the skin off his thumb and index finger as he thought and spoke, "We are not called to be saints. We are not called to be perfect. We are called to love. Amen."

"Well, those certainly are short, but profound. Thank you Billy. I have a difficult time with making up a sermon every week sometimes."

"St. Francis of Assisi is reported to have told his followers this: 'Preach the Gospel at all times. Use words if necessary.' I think you do that. You give us the right example of your sermons by your daily life," Billy encouraged; he was rubbing his fingers almost furiously together to help his words catch up with his thoughts.

"Do you think God is up in heaven or where is He?" was the next serious question from Taylor, always pushing Billy for more responses.

There was a longer pause as both listened to birds chirping and squirrels running through the tree next to them, otherwise it was very quiet.

"God could be this tiny speck, like a diamond, glowing inside of each of us. A brilliant light and love too great for words to describe. It is the 'I AM. YAHWEH. GOD. Hidden from yourself, but always there, always available. Hidden from the damaging, malicious, beastly, Free Will. Crowded down to a tiny speck because we fill ourselves with other things we think are important; like our plans, our materialistic accumulations, our pettiness. We should give Him more room to grow in us. We should let our 'Temple' be pure. You see some people do a better job at this than others. Some people, in their eyes—their windows—let some of that brilliant light of love burst out to share with others. God is in every one of us, and we should strive to find Him there and welcome Him home in our hearts."

Jimbo and Caroline

It probably was inevitable, but neither one really saw it coming. They were childhood friends; shared secrets and grief, then didn't see each other for years. They grew from children to young adults in the meantime. Then one day at a Bureau of Land Management auction of wild mustangs and burros....

"Ladies and Gentlemen, this mustang came from the mountains of Southern California where the grazing is too thin, he is a three year old gelding and looks to have some Quarter and Arabian blood in him. What is my opening bid?"

"$50," shouted a young woman with a blonde ponytail.

$75," Jimbo countered. He was interested in this horse and wanted to adopt him.

$100," she kept the bidding going.

"$150," he said, hoping to stop the bid and win the horse.

$200," she wasn't backing down.

$300." He was serious.

The two contestants glared at each other across the busy room. She had the blonde hair, blue-green eyes and those dimples. He had matured; grown taller, more muscular, dark brown hair, steel gray eyes, and was not a man to trifle with. After a moment there was a flicker of recognition. Caroline? He mouthed. Jimbo? She responded.

Bang.

"$300 gets this horse, goes to card # 56 over there."

The crowd drifted away. Caroline and Jimbo drifted towards each other.

"Looks like you got a horse," she said.

"I'll share it with you since you seemed to want him too. I didn't know it was you bidding."

"He is pretty. A paint. I don't know how to train a horse, do you?"

"Not really, but we can try it together if you want a challenge."

Jimbo and Caroline met every day for several weeks learning to train their wild mustang.

"Jimbo, I like this time with you," she said.

"I'm Jim now. I moved past Jimbo in about the 9th grade, he replied.

"Oh, changing names on me now. What other changes have gone on since I left the area then off to school?" she wanted to know.

Jim met often with Merle down at Lilly's to get advice on how to train a horse, and he learned the art of the easy, gentle method of horse training. Merle enjoyed being a teacher. Seems like Jim was always a student, always learning.

Jim and Caroline talked every day and the friendship and closeness they once had grew again. The mustang also made progress with their steady training. Jim wrote her a poem of sorts:

Indian Gentling

The Indians
Knew how.

They didn't
break their horses
or their spirit.

The Indians
gentled
their horse
with care
and nurturing,
trust
and understanding.

Indian gentling.
Gentle love.

And that is what
I've done
with you,
my love.

Caroline felt safe with Jim. He was a man of substance, someone who could take care of her. They spent
more time together. Katherine noticed.

"When are you going to bring 'Mystery Girl' home for your dad and I to meet her?"

"No rush Mom. Maybe this week end."

"Good, plan to have her come for dinner."

"Yes, ma'am."

Saturday was a bright, warm, Spring day. Katherine was weeding her garden. Caroline and Jim retuned from the barn where they had been grooming the mustang. Introductions were made and Caroline joined Katherine in the garden. Jim planned to head to Lilly's to talk again with Merle.

"Just pull the weeds around those peas."

"I'm afraid I'll pull the peas up not knowing a pea from a weed," Caroline replied.

"The weeds usually have a broader leaf and if you have a question, just ask me," Katherine coached.

"I like this. I like the feel of the dirt and the smell of it," Caroline was feeling like a farm hand.

"Yes, it grows on you, then gets in your blood where you can't wait to get out in the garden," Katherine said. "It isn't like work, it is more like therapy."

"Come on Caroline, enough dirt play." Jim had returned and was ready for something else.

They took a walk through the meadow, then the woods to the backside of Potts cemetery. Caroline went to her favorite spot by Aunt Mattie while Jim went to visit the Pattersons. It was like years ago as children when they first met. They didn't talk now, and each had their own thoughts, past and present, and trying to peek into the future. On the walk back home they held hands. After dinner Jim and Caroline walked over to his grandmother's empty house and sat on her porch swing. His father and mother moved to their own porch and their identical swing. The moon was rising, the night critters were making their noises, and the farm was in good shape.

Mother Earth.

Caroline leaned her head on Jim's strong shoulder as he held her hand. Everything was right with the world and he offered up a quick prayer of thanksgiving and hope.

Prayer.

"Jim I like this Caroline of yours. She is a smart girl. Do you think she is the one?" Katherine was curious about the relationship.

"Mom, she is the best girl I have ever dated. I'm new to this love thing, but I know I want to be around her all the time," he replied. "Oh and she is my best friend."

"Maybe Grandpa's journal will have some advice for you. I sure don't have any."

Jim, went to his room to find his treasure:

TOM REED

Love

At some point you will find a friendship grow deeper and you will call it love. The Bible has many passages about love and you should find them, I suggest you start with my favorite at 1st Corinthians 13:4-7

"Love is patient and kind; love is not jealous or boastful; it is not arrogant or rude. Love does not insist on its own way; it is not irritable or resentful; it does not rejoice at wrong, but rejoices at right. Love bears all things, believes all things, hopes all things, endures all things."

Ending

There was a wedding in Cedar Grove that year. The ceremony was held behind the Patterson home looking out over their land. The Rev. John Taylor officiated. Families from the area came. Jim noticed Lem Potts and his new bride, Mark and Melinda, Burton Johnson and his daughter. Burton even wore a pair of new coveralls. All the boys from Lilly's were there. Bobby and Clarence kept waving like cheerleaders with pompoms. Merle was standing straight and tall in the present moment, happy. John Sloan, the land owner, nodded to him. The Co-op and John Deere men were also mingling about. Billy Berkley tucked his helmet under one of his arms and kept his wide grin going to everyone while he snapped pictures. Jim realized how blessed he was with these friends.

Jim and Caroline continued in the Patterson tradition of farming and taking care of the land.

God is good.

Note to reader

This was a complex undertaking by trying to weave in so many different stories and time lines and not confuse the reader with too many times and characters. I needed help and editors. Several friends and readers of my previous books graciously took the time to preview this book and offer their thoughts. I know I'll miss many names who read the manuscript at various phases, and I apologize for any oversights there. Those I can think of now include: the invaluable editor, Rene Holt. Bob Flynn, Angie Baggett, Brenda Whalley, Jil Burks Cooper, Judy Truex Reed, Jim Moss, Randal McPheeters, Margaret Hopper, and many others. This group took very rough manuscript drafts and helped refine them into a readable book for you.

Since I'm thanking folks, I want to circle back and thank the Johnny Robinson family for letting me tell their story, even in a fictional form, but I always admired their courageous love for the land and daily hard work on it. The Pattersons don't exist, but the Robinsons certainly do.

Other books of fiction by Tom Reed include:

Truthful Moments, a story of a veteran suffering from post traumatic stress disorder witnesses a murder, which triggers flashbacks from his wartime. As he untangles his past from the present, he helps solve the murder. This book was selected to be in the 2011 Southern Festival of Books.

Innocence Killed, A story based on a true "cold case" involving a cast of characters on a small Southern college campus where a coed was murdered. After 15 years the case remains unsolved, but is solved in this book.

CPSIA information can be obtained at www.ICGtesting.com
Printed in the USA
LVOW08s1454260914

406067LV00001B/30/P